JULIE LAWSON

THE GHOST OF AVALANCHE MOUNTAIN

Stoddart Kids

TORONTO • NEW YORK

Published in Canada in 2000 by
Stoddart Kids,
a division of Stoddart Publishing Co. Limited
34 Lesmill Road
Toronto, Canada M3B 2T6
Tel (416) 445-3333 Fax (416) 445-5967
E-mail cservice@genpub.com

Published in the United States in 2000 by
Stoddart Kids,
a division of Stoddart Publishing Co. Limited
180 Varick Street, 9th Floor
New York, New York 10014
Toll free 1-800-805-1083
E-mail gdsinc@genpub.com

Distributed in Canada by
General Distribution Services
325 Humber College Blvd.
Toronto, Canada M9W 7C3
Tel (416) 213-1919 Fax (416) 213-1917
E-mail cservice@genpub.com

Distributed in the United States by
General Distribution Services, PMB 128
4500 Witmer Industrial Estates
Niagara Falls, New York 14305-3876
Toll free 1-800-805-1083
E-mail gdsinc@genpub.com

Canadian Cataloguing in Publication Data

Julie Lawson, 1947 –
The ghost of Avalanche Mountain

ISBN 0-7737-6091-1
I Title.
PS8573.A94G46 2000   jC813'.54   C99-932577-9
PZ7.L43Gh 2000

Book and cover design by Tannice Goddard
Cover illustration by Ken Campbell

We acknowledge for their financial support of our publishing program the Government of Canada through the Book Publishing Industry Development Program (BPIDP), the Canada Council, and the Ontario Arts Council.

Printed and bound in Canada

For my brother, Chris Goodwin

Acknowledgements

Many individuals assisted in my research for this book. I would especially like to thank the following:

The Revelstoke and District Historical Association, and particularly the curator, Catherine English, who read the manuscript in its entirety; Pat Dunn, Outreach Officer, Mount Revelstoke and Glacier National Parks, who provided answers to specific bird questions, as well as information on the plants and wildlife of the area; Jim Buckingham and Don Waters, who read the chapters pertaining to the avalanche and provided invaluable comments on backcountry skiing and avalanche safety; and Mary Buckingham, who helped clarify the intricacies of backcountry skiing.

Thanks to Dianne Martin, teacher-librarian of Big Eddy Elementary and Columbia Park Elementary Schools, and to the many children of Revelstoke who wrote letters giving me a "kid's-eye view" of their town, especially Chelsie, Kayleigh, Lindsay, Steven, Jakob, and Kyle.

I'm grateful to my friend Carol Delisle, whose comments about past and present gave me much to think about; to my editors, Kathryn Cole and Lynne Missen, for their insightful and perceptive comments; and to my husband, Patrick, for sharing many inspiring journeys to the Selkirk Mountains and Glacier National Park.

Finally, a heartfelt thank you to my father, whose chance remark prompted a completely new vision for this book. I wish he could have lived to see the trilogy come full circle.

Prologue

From the diary of Karin Anderson Warren . . .

Revelstoke, BC
November 1920

 I have read that "goldstone" is not a stone at all, nor is it any kind of mined mineral. It is made from aventurine glass, spangled close and fine with particles of sparkling material like copper shavings or gold flakes. It was first made in monasteries in Italy, a far cry from our Selkirk Mountains. But it came to our mountains nonetheless, and one small goldstone marble somehow found its way into a pedlar's basket. From there it ended up in my mother's hands. And then into mine.

 But what of before? Long before the pedlar and his basket, someone created the goldstone. Someone mixed gold and copper into the sand, applied the heat, and shaped the stone. Someone stirred in the magic. How? And why? It doesn't really matter. But Mama was right all those years ago. The goldstone is a magic stone, for dreaming the future.

I have dreamed of the child who will have the goldstone when I am gone. Still further into the future, I have dreamed of a girl named Ashley. Strange name for a girl, Ashley. And ever since I moved back to the Selkirks, the dreams have been strange. As if a mysterious force is at work, here in the mountains . . .

1

THE PAST

Jonathan could hardly remember the time before the lightning.

He knew he'd had a mother who died. And a father, who'd taken him by train to the mountains and left him with Grandfather Silver. Jonathan was seven years old at the time. He never saw his father again.

The months that followed had been a blur of birds and animals and trees and flowers and Grandfather telling him the names of everything. And telling him, Watch out for the spirits of the mountains and the Great Glacier because you never know when they're watching. You never know when they'll test you. So

3

remember to say your prayers. And when you're a little bit older, then you can help with the glass.

The glass was a blur of heat and sand and swirling flakes of gold, stirred and shaped into the special marbles Grandfather called "the goldstones." And the monthly treks to the village to get supplies and sell the goldstones — that, too, was a blur.

Everything was a blur. Until the day of the lightning.

It was summer. The air was hot. White clouds hung in the sky. The birds were quiet, the flowers in the alpine meadow were still. Everything was hushed and waiting.

Not Grandfather. He was finishing a new batch of goldstones, anxious to take them to the village that day. "Feels like a storm," he remarked, but that didn't stop him. Back and forth he went, from the furnace in the shed to the cooling tray in the meadow. Back and forth, from fire to ice, with Jonathan at his heels.

And the whole time it was talk, talk, talk, a blur of questions and answers about gold and ice and mountains and spirits and why things were the way they were.

"Can I be a glass-maker like you?" Jonathan asked. "Will you teach me to make the goldstones?"

"Reckon I might," Grandfather said. "But there's an art to it, you know." He picked two marbles out of the glacial ice and held them up against the sky, one in each hand. "You see any difference?"

Jonathan looked closely, then pointed to the one in Grandfather's left hand. "This one's darker," he said.

"I added an extra bit of copper, that's why,"

Grandfather explained. "It gives it more of a reddish tone. And the cullet I mixed in, those pieces of broken glass? That glass was a rusty red, which also accounts for the color. Now, you notice anything about the gold?"

"The other marble, the one in your right hand, it's got way more gold. So it's brighter."

"There you go. You play around a bit, you change the effect. Now, see how dark the sky's getting? That'll change the color, too. And make the gold look different."

The clouds were looming over the mountains, huge and black with warning, but Jonathan barely gave them a glance. "Where does all the gold come from?"

"Panned it myself, a thousand years ago," Grandfather said. "'Course I might be exaggerating, time-wise. But it doesn't take much to make a goldstone. What I've got left'll last me another thousand years."

Jonathan's small face scrunched up with worry. "Will there be enough for me?"

"Oh, I reckon you've got a right bright future, my son. But look at that sky now! The spirits are angry about something. And see how the goldstone's changing?"

Jonathan looked up and saw a gleam of gold against the dark purple sky. He was about to speak when an explosive crash ripped through the quiet. Booming echoes rolled over the mountains. A giant spark jumped from the top of the cloud to the bottom.

"Down, down!" Grandfather was shouting. "Get down!"

Before Jonathan could move, another spark jumped, this time from the thunderhead looming above Avalanche Mountain. Spellbound, he watched the spark leap through the air and blaze a jagged path from sky to earth — searching for the highest point, the quickest way to the ground, and finding it — in Grandfather's outstretched hand.

Between the lightning and the thunder, Jonathan grew a thousand years older. Or so it seemed. He looked at his grandfather lying motionless on the ground and knew he had to do something. But what? Had Grandfather told him what to do if struck by lightning?

A blur of remedies sharpened and clicked into focus. Cures for coughs and corns, earaches and chilblains, headaches and frostbite and indigestion. But lightning?

Water, Jonathan remembered. Cold water. And salt.

He ran into the cabin, found the bag of salt, and carried it outside to the cooling tray. He poured salt over the slushy ice, then scooped up the mixture and packed it around Grandfather, over his face, over his neck and chest, over his scorched right arm and blackened fingers. When the ice was gone, and the salt, he filled a bucket with water from the nearby stream and poured it over his grandfather.

It made sense. Lightning was fire. Water put out fire. So water had to put out lightning.

He begged Grandfather to wake up, to open his eyes, to say something. He prayed to the spirits, "Please don't be angry. Please wake him up. Please . . ."

Finally Grandfather coughed and sputtered and opened his eyes. With Jonathan's help, he managed to stagger to his feet and into the cabin. There he struggled out of his wet clothes and, gritting his teeth against the pain, lay down on his bunk.

"Serves me right," he gasped. "I saw it coming. I felt a tingle in the back of my head, see. I should've crouched down right then and there, but, oh, no, I wait too long and the lightning goes straight into my hand and down my arm. My arm's burning and I see it drop like it isn't even a part of me. Then the current crosses through to my left leg and bolts out through my foot. And leaves behind this terrible fierce pain.

"Then the pain, it turns into something warm and peaceful. Like I'm thrown into a soft white cotton ball, and everything's so bright I can hardly see. I feel myself floating away to another place . . . But I hear my old heart start to beat, and that's when I know I'm still here."

He cast a sorrowful look at his hand and sighed. "Jonathan, my son, I reckon you're my right hand now. So listen carefully . . . I'll tell you what you have to do." When he finished speaking, he closed his eyes and fell into a deep sleep.

The goldstones that had been cooling in the ice had scattered in Jonathan's frenzied attempt to cure his grandfather. He now set himself the task of finding them so he could take them to the village as planned. Supplies were needed and, more importantly, ointments and bandages for Grandfather's arm.

What had once been a blur of trails and tracks was now a clear map in Jonathan's mind. Follow the path through the alpine meadow and forest until you come to Glacier House. Then hike along the tracks to the village.

The train schedules were clear, too. He didn't have to worry about being surprised in a tunnel or on one of the trestles towering above the creeks.

He wasn't afraid when he reached the village. Grandfather had told him where to go, who to see, and what to say. In no time at all, he was on his way home.

As he hiked up the mountain trail, Jonathan thought about what had happened. He remembered Grandfather once telling him that the spirits liked to test a person's mettle. Perhaps that was why the lightning had struck. The spirits were testing him. Since Grandfather was alive, he must have passed the test. The spirits had been watching. They'd answered his prayers.

Back in the cabin, he found Grandfather sitting up in bed, his face aglow with excitement. "I was asleep and dreaming, Jonathan. And in my dream there's a goldstone with a dazzling light. And when I wake up, here it is." He opened his good hand to show Jonathan. "See this? You didn't take them all to the village!"

"No, Grandfather. You were holding it so tight I didn't want to take it away. I — I'm sorry."

Grandfather didn't seem to mind. "In my dream, in this goldstone light, there are faces. Faces I've never seen before. Names I don't know. Voices I've never heard. And they're all telling me something about the future."

Jonathan frowned, puzzled.

"Don't you see? Something happened when the lightning struck. The charge shot straight through me and into the goldstones. It struck them with magic, my son! Magic from the spirits of Avalanche Mountain! You saw it, didn't you? How the lightning streaked from the mountain and seared into my right hand? And the other goldstone —" He stopped abruptly. "Where is the other one, the one I was holding up to the sky? The one that took hold of the charge?"

Jonathan gulped. He'd seen that goldstone fall from his grandfather's hand the instant he was struck. He must have picked it up with the others. He'd searched carefully, even amongst the wildflowers where some of the marbles had rolled and been concealed. He had found them all, taken them to the village, and sold them to the pedlar. "That — that other one," he stammered. "It's — it's gone. I'm s-sorry." His throat thickened with tears.

Grandfather wasn't angry. "Never mind," he said, patting Jonathan's hand. "I reckon one powerful goldstone's enough. I'm still here, that's the main thing."

Jonathan's heart agreed, but his mind told him this was another test. "I'll find the other goldstone," he said. "I'll bring it back. I promise." He vowed he would keep his promise. It would make his grandfather so happy he would never go away. Unlike Jonathan's mother and father, he would stay with Jonathan forever.

2

In the shadow of the Great Glacier, Jonathan turned eight. And nine. And ten . . .

Soon he lost count of the years and no longer cared. His life was a rhythm of mountains and seasons. Of day and night, sun and cloud, snow and ice.

When he heard his first avalanche, the winter after the lightning strike, he thought the world was coming to an end. The boom shook the mountains, brought on the wind, and then the river of snow.

"The spirits are angry," Grandfather had said calmly. "Sometimes they send the lightning, sometimes the avalanche. Sometimes they even ride the avalanche and drag the trees alongside to help them steer. That's why you never see a tree standing straight and tall on an avalanche path. All because of those angry spirits."

Jonathan wondered why the spirits were angry. Was it something he'd done? Was it because of the gold-stone he'd sold by mistake? That had to be the reason. It made him all the more determined to find it.

Once a month Jonathan made his way to the village. Grandfather usually accompanied him, although his legs were still shaky from the lightning strike and his eyes somewhat sensitive to light. They traveled by foot or by snowshoe, depending on the season. Over the alpine meadow then down through the forest, through the heavy scent of hemlock and cedar, weaving their way through the massive trees that Grandfather compared to the pillars of ancient cathedrals. When they reached the railway line at Glacier House, they set off along the tracks, following the steel ribbon through evergreen canyons, in and out of tunnels, over high wooden trestles, and along the river until they reached the village.

They didn't linger in the village. They bought supplies, collected empty bottles and pieces of broken glass, and gathered the bits of coal that spilled from the tenders of passing trains. They also sold their goldstones to the pedlar. He, in turn, took them on board the trains and sold them as souvenirs to the ever-growing number of tourists.

Grandfather liked the idea of the goldstones going across the country, maybe even across the ocean to far distant places. He liked to think that some might end up in Italy, where he himself had traveled as a young man. Maybe one would end up in the remote Italian monastery where he had long ago learned the art of making the goldstones.

Jonathan hoped it wouldn't be the one he vowed to find, because he never wanted to leave the mountains. He fixed his eyes on their peaks as he made his way home, and whispered their names as a chant. Uto, Eagle, Avalanche . . . And shining in their midst, the Great Glacier. The beacon over his home.

As soon as the journey was over, Jonathan set to work making a new batch of goldstones. He fed the coal to the furnace in Grandfather's glass-making shed, waited until the fireclay pot was roaring hot, then poured in sand, soda-ash, limestone, and bits of recycled glass.

Everything melted together in the heat of the fire. When the molten glass was oozing like thick honey, Jonathan sprinkled in the flakes of copper and gold. Sometimes more, sometimes less. Sometimes he merely shook the gold dust from his fingers.

The next step was to shape the goldstones. Following Grandfather's instructions, Jonathan dipped a long, hollow pipe into the molten glass, collected a small glob, and gently blew through the pipe until the glob became a perfect sphere. One at a time, he broke the marbles off the end of the pipe, then took them outside to harden and cool.

Jonathan took pride in his work. He knew his grandfather was pleased. He was Grandfather's right hand. He was the light of his life.

3

THE PAST

One dark winter's day Grandfather said, "Well, Jonathan Silver, you're now fifteen. Almost a man by my reckoning. You can dream your future if you've a mind."

Jonathan couldn't imagine a future any different, or better, than his present. But to *know*! To have that power, that sense of being close to the spirits, of being a part of something beyond this world.

Grandfather had often spoken of his goldstone dreams. "They're like mist on the mountains," he said. "You know something's behind the mist but you can't quite make it out. Then the wind brushes by or the sunlight breaks through and you have a clear picture. But it only lasts for a second, and it's near impossible to remember."

Jonathan had one hope, that his dreams would be clear enough to show him where the other special goldstone might be found. But once he began to dream, he realized that Grandfather was right. The dreams were like mist on the mountains.

One dream showed him a woman wearing the goldstone as a pendant. Jonathan barely had a glimpse before she disappeared.

In a later dream he saw the goldstone embedded in ice. He knew it was close. It hadn't gone to Italy or across the country. It had stayed in his mountains. If he kept on dreaming, he was sure to discover where it was.

But it was not to be. Over that long winter, and the summer that followed, the dreams remained a mist and the whereabouts of the goldstone, a mystery. It was lost and found. Then lost again.

Jonathan caught brief glimpses of it, once in a quiet town by the sea, then in a land where north was south and night was day, a land he couldn't comprehend.

One night, when Jonathan was beginning to give up hope, the dreams pulled him back to the mountains. A clear image broke through the mist. He saw a girl moving across the snow through splashes of color — yellows and purples and blues, like wildflowers blooming out of season. The way the girl was dressed reminded him of columbine, coral-red with a touch of bright yellow. What he saw next made Jonathan's heart beat faster. In his dream, the girl's face was lit up by the sun. And shining at her throat was the goldstone.

He woke up, every nerve on edge. The earlier dreams — none of them mattered. He now knew the face of the person he had to find.

A few months later, he dreamed the name.

When Grandfather failed to wake up one morning, Jonathan knew there was no cure that would revive him. Nor was there a remedy that would soften the ache in his heart.

He wrapped his grandfather in a blanket and carried him, through howling wind and swirling snow, to the edge of the Great Glacier. Then, as Grandfather had wished, he placed him in a deep crevasse in the ice.

In the shadow of the Glacier, Jonathan repeated the vow he'd made as a child. "I'll find the other gold-stone. I'll bring it back. I promise." He knew the spirits were watching.

He returned to the cabin and prepared for his journey down the mountain. He left everything as it was, a blur of glass and flakes of gold. As soon as his promise was kept, he would return.

His plan was a map in his mind. Follow the tracks past the village and into the town of Revelstoke. Look for a family called Ashley. Then find their fair-haired daughter.

He would begin his search at the railway yards. Locomotives burned coal. Burning meant ashes. Hence the name. Mr. Ashley had to be a fireman who stoked coal on one of the tenders.

Except, Jonathan realized, his own name, Silver, had nothing to do with gold or glass. He might be on the wrong track. But he had to start somewhere.

It was evening by the time he reached the railway yards. He was surprised by all the activity. Dozens of men were rushing about with shovels and torches. A locomotive with the steam up, ready to go, was rumbling on the tracks. Before Jonathan had a chance to ask about the Ashleys, two official-looking men approached him and said they could use an extra pair of hands. Why? To help clear the tracks, after yet another blasted avalanche. Did he want to sign on? If so, he'd better hurry. The train was about to pull out.

Jonathan said he'd like to sign on, but couldn't, since he didn't know how to read or write.

The men laughed in a friendly way, then told him to grab a shovel and hop on the crew car. They'd take care of the signing-on later. Right now they needed all the help they could get.

Jonathan knew about being helpful. And maybe someone in the crew would know the Ashleys.

Within minutes he found himself heading back up the line, to the summit of Rogers Pass, to the shadow of the Glacier he'd left only hours before. It was his second time on a train. He was sixteen years old, and his life was about to change forever.

4

THE PRESENT

The parcel arrived by special delivery on August the first.

Eleven-year-old Ashley Gillespie had been expecting it. Two weeks earlier she'd received an e-mail from her Aunt Jo with the subject, SAUTEED SNAIL WITH A COUPLE OF LEEKS. The message had been short and to the point. *Happy Birthday!*

It hadn't taken Ashley long to decipher her aunt's rhyming code. After experimenting with *sail* and *tale*, she'd settled on *mail*. *Leeks* rhymed with *weeks*. So the message meant that her birthday present was in the mail and would arrive in two weeks. And here it was, right on schedule, delivered to her door as she and her parents were finishing a late breakfast.

"From Dances with Whales?" Ashley's father teased. Any mention of his sister, Jo, was accompanied by some kind of wisecrack, although his tone could never disguise his admiration. Especially since Jo, known throughout the world as Joanne Gillespie, was a mystery writer whose books sold in the millions. She had also been part of a whale rescue operation, and, ever since, Ashley's father had jokingly called her "Dances with Whales."

"Feels pretty light," he said, weighing the parcel in his hands. "Dances with Whales really saved on postage this time."

"She's not Dances with Whales," Ashley scolded. "She's your famous sister."

"Is that a fact?" Dad grinned and handed back the parcel with its array of Australian stamps. "Any clues? Or is it just something wonderful?"

"Something wonderful," Ashley's mother remarked. "As always."

It was true. Over the years Ashley had received hand-painted boomerangs, a didgeridoo, shells from Tasmania, the shed skin of a gecko, and feathers from the brightly colored lorikeets found in Jo's own backyard. Ashley treasured such gifts, not only because they came from so far away, but also because they offered some insights into the aunt she'd never met.

The previous year Jo had sent her a modem so they could communicate by e-mail. She'd found it strange at first, telling her aunt the news of the day when in Australia it was already tomorrow. From the Down Under perspective, Ashley was always stuck in yesterday.

Still, she loved writing to her aunt. She wrote about everything — her home, the river, the mountains, the weather, and the town of Revelstoke where she'd lived her whole life. She wrote about school, how she was pretty good at everything except for spelling. She wrote about her best friend, Erica, who had an annoying habit of biting her nails but could faint on demand. And her second best friend, a boy called Raven, who stored a million useless facts in what passed for a brain. Like the names of famous people who shared Ashley's birthday, including himself.

Thoughts, ideas, feelings — anything that came into Ashley's mind spilled onto the screen and, with a click, vanished into cyberspace.

It was like communicating with a ghost, except that the ghost wrote back. Not in boring everyday English, but in rhyming code. And best of all, the ghost sent presents.

"Earth to Ashley." Mom waved a hand in front of Ashley's face. "Shall I put it away for your birthday?"

"That's three weeks away," Ashley protested. "I'm going to open it right now." She ripped off the brown paper and uncovered a box wrapped in silver paper. She shook it, but there wasn't a sound.

"Must be a spider web," Dad joked. "Can't get much quieter than that."

The present turned out to be a wooden box. "I bet there's something inside," Ashley said, but when she opened the lid she found nothing more than several layers of red and orange tissue paper.

"It's not only quiet, but invisible," Dad said. "Did Jo send you a code to figure that out?"

"Oh, Dad." Ashley crumpled the silver wrapping paper and tossed it at his head. "I wish Auntie Jo'd write a murder mystery with *you* as the victim."

"On that note, I better go. I may not be as famous as my sister, but the train won't leave without me." He bent down and kissed Ashley on the cheek. "Can't wait to find out how this mystery is solved. Of course, there may not be a mystery. Jo might have a case of writer's block. Your present might be just a plain old wooden box."

"It's hardly plain," Mom pointed out. "Look how beautifully it's made. All different strips of wood, see? But you can hardly notice the seams."

"Yeah, Dad. And there's nothing wrong with a box. I can keep jewelry in it, or letters, or all my Australia stuff, like stamps and shells and feathers. The thing is, it's not like Auntie Jo to send a box with tissue paper. It's totally out of character."

After saying good-bye to her dad, Ashley took another look inside the box. She removed the tissue, one layer at a time, and eventually discovered a note the size of a postage stamp. "I knew it, Mom! See this? It was hidden in the tissue. I practically need a magnifying glass to read it, but I think it says, 'The future is coming.' What do you think that means?"

Mom shrugged and reached for her jacket. "You know your aunt, honey. She's pretty cryptic. But I'll have to leave you to it. I'm working at the museum all day and I'll be home — wait a minute. You're going up Mount Revelstoke today, aren't you? With Erica and Raven and so forth? And her mom's driving?"

"Yes, yes . . ."

"Have you got everything?"

"Yes! See my pack sitting here? I'm all set."

"Right then! I'll be home around 4:00, unless the museum gets overly busy." She nodded at the present. "Good luck with the clues. And have fun on your hike. Have you got your notebook? I want a list of wild-flowers, and your dad'll want the birds."

"Forget it! I'm not even taking my binoculars. I'm just going for fun."

"With Raven spouting off a fact a minute?" Mom raised her eyebrows and they both laughed.

As soon as Mom left, Ashley went back to the note. *The future is coming.* Was there a rhyme involved? What rhymed with *future*? Or *coming*? Maybe *come*? *Gum, mum, strum* . . .

Maybe it meant there was another present. She shook the box again and this time heard a soft thud. "Aha!" she exclaimed. "There *is* something else!"

Just then the doorbell rang and a familiar voice called out, "Hey, Ash! Are you there? Wake up, it's 10:00! Time to go!" The words were accompanied by more ringing and a rhythmical knocking at the door.

Ashley reluctantly put down the box and picked up her pack.

Erica was at the door, her short dark hair a tangle of curls, her fluorescent purple nails chipped with impatience. "Took you long enough," she said. "Are you ready? Raven's in the car and we just have to pick up Clipper and Steph."

A few minutes later they were winding up the Meadow in the Sky Parkway in Mount Revelstoke National Park. It was one of Ashley's favorite spots, especially in July and August when the alpine flowers exploded in fields of red, yellow, and blue. But as she and her friends hiked the trails around the summit, she found herself paying little attention to the spectacular scenery around her. She paid even less attention to Raven's relentless accounting of wildlife facts.

"Did you guys know there's thirty-one different kinds of song sparrows? Thirty-one! And chickadees — you know there's four kinds right here in the park? So keep your eyes and ears peeled for chickadees. The mountain chickadee has a white eyebrow, and the boreal's kind of all brown and sounds like a black-capped with a cold. The black-capped has a black cap and the chestnut-backed has a chestnut back."

"Makes sense," said Steph.

Clipper belched in agreement.

"We might see all four today," Raven said. "Except the black-capped and chestnut —"

"Stop!" Erica gave him a playful whack on the shoulder. "God, Raven, why do we ever let you come? You are so boring! And how do you ever see a bird or anything when you talk so much? A chickadee's a chickadee's a chickadee! Whoa! Say that seven times real fast. A chickadee's a chick — oh, forget it. You're awfully quiet, Ashley. For a change. Isn't she, Steph?

How come?"

"Well, if you must know . . ." Ashley told them about her aunt's mysterious present.

Erica's reaction was typical. "The future is coming? Well, *duhh*. Like it'll be here tomorrow, right? Jeez, Ash. That's hardly a mystery."

True. But Ashley knew her aunt well enough to know there was more to a message than a collection of words. She couldn't wait to get home and examine the box more closely.

5

THE PAST

In the shadow of the Glacier, Jonathan watched and waited.

He could no longer remember the time before the lightning. Only what came after — the time between the fire and the ice. The time before the avalanche.

He shimmered into the trains, into the billowing clouds of steam, and into the glare of the firebox. He shimmered through passenger cars and stations. He shimmered into the mountains and along the river. Watching, waiting for the Ashley girl.

He shimmered into the places of his childhood — the dining room at Glacier House, where Grandfather had treated him to his first taste of chocolate, and the village, where they had collected the colored glass to make the goldstones.

He shimmered into Golden and Revelstoke, the towns on either side of the pass. He didn't like the towns. He never had. They were full of shrieks and clatters, rumbles, squeals, and roars. And shouts. He remembered the village youths and how they'd tormented him with names. *Hermit. Lunatic.* Names hurled at an old man and a small boy, holding tightly to each other's hands.

That was long ago. Like the vaguely remembered mother and father, the grandfather and the boy were gone. All that remained was the goldstone. And the Ashley.

He remembered his dreams. Remembered seeing bright flashes of the Ashley near the Glacier, her slight figure dressed in red, like columbine flowering in the snow. He remembered seeing her at the summit of Rogers Pass, her hair the color of an aspen leaf in autumn.

He shimmered in a strange, shadowy world of past and present. The only future he knew was the one he had already dreamed.

The years passed and still Jonathan waited.

Watching, waiting for the Ashley.

One summer's day, he tasted something almost tangible. It was a yearning, a feeling so powerful it drew him over the tracks and into the town of Revelstoke. When he reached the station he was surprised to find himself in the midst of a large and happy crowd, gathered around an eastbound train.

A young couple was standing arm in arm beside the locomotive. The woman held a bouquet of yellow roses and pearly everlasting, but these weren't the only flowers. At the front of the engine, someone had placed an enormous wreath of purplish-blue lupine and crimson paintbrush, arranged in the shape of a heart. There was a colorful banner, too, though Jonathan couldn't make out the words.

It didn't matter. He knew why he was there. He saw it, gleaming on the white lace of the woman's dress. The goldstone!

His excitement quickly gave way to confusion. Was that woman the Ashley? She couldn't be. She had blonde hair and blue eyes like the girl in his dream, but her age was wrong. Unless . . . Was it possible his dream was wrong?

No matter. The waiting was over. The goldstone was within his grasp.

He stepped up to the woman, intent on snatching the goldstone from the chain around her neck. He reached out his hand —

And she walked right through him. Right through him, as if he wasn't there. Radiant with happiness, she threw her bouquet into the crowd and a cry rang out. "Three cheers for Karin and Stuart! Hip, hip, hurray! Hip, hip, hurray!"

Oh, the noise! The screech of the whistle, the shuddering roar of the locomotive. The cheers and laughter and hearty calls as the couple boarded the train. "Hurray! Congratulations! Bon voyage!"

Jonathan was about to shut his ears to the clamor when he heard a child ask, "Where's Miss Anderson going?"

"She's Mrs. Warren now, dear," a lady answered. "She's off on her honeymoon."

Honeymoon? Jonathan didn't understand. Warren? Anderson?

There wasn't an Ashley. Only the goldstone. And now it was gone.

Jonathan watched in despair as the train belched out a cloud of cinders and rumbled out of the station.

It didn't work, Grandfather. The shimmer didn't work.
You'll have to try harder.
Harder? How can I try harder?
Wait awhile. Sleep awhile.
I've been waiting for years. How much longer?
Sleep until you're ready. Sleep until the shimmer wakes you.

Jonathan felt a rush of panic.

Where do I sleep?
You know, Jonathan. In the place they made for you.
I don't like it there. It doesn't even have my name on it. And it's too far from home. Can't I sleep with you?
Of course, my son. But if you do, you'll never shimmer back to the world. You'll never find the goldstone.
I made a promise.

I know. But I don't hold you to it. Come home with me and sleep.

I can't. All I ever gave you was that promise.

That's not true, my son. You were my goldstone. My right hand. You were the light of my life.

Many years passed.

One day Jonathan shimmered to Glacier House and was surprised to find it abandoned. He discovered two vandals demolishing the rooms, carrying off glass bottles and lamps and china, even porcelain chamber pots and hot water jugs.

Jonathan wanted to stop them. He shimmered harder, trying to give himself shape and form and substance. Then he lunged toward one of the vandals and drove him into the wall.

Or thought he had. The vandal, a burly hulk of a man, passed through him like air, like the woman at the station had done. Only this time the hulk cried out in pain and hollered, "Whadja go 'n' do that for?"

"Do what?" The other man turned, his arms full of loot.

"Hit me in the back, right smack in the kidneys! Almost knocked me offa my feet!"

"Did no such thing! How could I, from halfway across the room?"

"Well, there's no one else in sight, is there?"

"No, but it sure as heck wasn't me."

The hulk looked over his shoulder and frowned. Was that a shadow on the wall? He shook his head and rubbed the small of his back. "Crazy fool place," he muttered.

He didn't see Jonathan smile. He didn't hear him shout, *It's happening, Grandfather! I'm beginning to come back to the world.*

As time went on, Jonathan learned to appear and disappear, in a flash of bright light or in a pale purple glow. He startled small animals. He flushed birds out of hiding. He stalked the solitary hikers who ventured near the Glacier, then lured them away with flickers of light. He shimmered through the pass from the summit to the valleys. And all the while, he watched and waited for the Ashley.

The summit changed. The trains went underground. A new highway followed the old railway line, carrying vehicles the likes of which Jonathan had never imagined. Snowsheds protected the highway from avalanche paths, as they had once protected the railway tracks. But the snowsheds were now built of concrete, hundreds of feet long. And instead of wooden trestles, steel and concrete structures towered above the creeks.

One summer morning, as Jonathan was shimmering along the highway, he felt the same powerful yearning that had once drawn him to the Revelstoke station. This time it pulled him to the summit of Rogers Pass.

A family was taking photographs. There was a mother and father, a boy and a girl. The girl was close to Jonathan's age. And she was wearing the goldstone.

The instant he saw it, Jonathan knew it was the one.

It gleamed, it shone, it beckoned. All he needed was a flash of light to startle the girl, a tug at the chain, and the goldstone would be in his hand.

He could hardly restrain himself. The waiting was over. At last he had found the Ashley.

But wait . . . This girl was younger than the woman he'd seen in Revelstoke, but she was still older than the Ashley in his dream. And her appearance was wrong. Her hair wasn't blonde, it was light brown. And when she shifted her gaze from the camera he could see the eyes were wrong. They were green, with flecks of brown. They were supposed to be blue.

The dream was wrong. But it had led him to the goldstone, and that's all that mattered. This time he wouldn't rush in. He would wait until the girl was away from the others, then summon the force that would enable him to take the goldstone. He would do it so quickly, so smoothly, she would not even know it was gone until it was too late.

The family seemed to be a happy one, although the boy was showing signs of impatience. "Can't we go now?" he said. "This is taking forever."

The father handed him the camera. "Here, Ian, why don't you take one more picture? Take it so Avalanche Mountain is in the background. I'll squeeze in between Jo and your mom."

"OK, everybody," the boy said. "Say cheese!"

Say *cheese*? It was very strange. And *Jo*? It didn't sound anything like *Ashley*. But it was unmistakably the goldstone.

After the picture was taken, the mother and father and boy wandered across the parking lot to look at a large map of the area. The girl bent down to tie her shoelace, then got up to join the others.

Now, thought Jonathan. Now's the time. He stepped in her path, summoned a charge, and felt the light tingle through to his fingertips. He was reaching out to take hold of the goldstone when the girl suddenly moved back a few steps. "What . . .?" she whispered. "What is this?"

"You can see me!" Jonathan exclaimed. "Can you hear me? You're not the Ashley but it doesn't matter. I've come for the goldstone. Give it to me."

The girl frowned as if she didn't understand.

Jonathan tried again. "Give me the goldstone."

Unexpectedly the girl began to yell. "Hey, Ian! Mom, Dad! Come see this! It must be —"

"What, a bear?" The boy was already at her side. "Did you see a bear? There's supposed to be grizzlies up here."

"No, some kind of firefly. Do you see the light? Can you hear that humming sound?"

"Must be time for lunch," the father said. "Jo's imagination is running wild."

"It was a strange humming light," she insisted as they were walking away. "I even felt it! I probably got bitten. Can you see a mark, Mom? Right here on my throat? I'll probably itch for the next three days. I'll probably break out in a rash."

As the family was getting into their car, the girl turned around. She looked directly at the spot where

Jonathan was standing and gave an exclamation of surprise. Then she shook her head and got into the car with the others.

Jonathan stood at the side of the highway, desolate and confused. Once again he'd had the goldstone within his grasp. Once again he'd lost it.

I failed Grandfather. I tried to come back to the world. It didn't work. She didn't see me. She didn't hear me.

She's not the one.

But she had the goldstone.

She's not the one. The time has not yet come.

I don't understand.

Forget the goldstone, Jonathan. Come home.

I made a promise.

Then have patience, my son. And trust in the dream.

6

THE PRESENT

It was late afternoon by the time Ashley got home from
Mount Revelstoke. She thanked Erica's mom, waved
good-bye to her friends, and raced inside with one
thought in her mind. Her aunt's present.

She picked up the box, gave it a vigorous shake, and
once again heard the soft thud. OK, Ashley, this is it . . .

She examined the lid, the sides, the bottom. She ran
her finger along the seams. She felt the smooth wood,
jiggled the latch, pressed the hinges. Then she noticed
that one strip of wood was slightly smoother than the
rest. She pressed along its length. At the halfway mark
she thought she heard a faint click. With rising excite-

ment, she pressed more firmly. Her persistence paid off. The bottom of the box sprung open and revealed a tiny secret compartment.

Ashley wiggled in a finger and pulled out a ball of crumpled orange tissue. Was it one of Auntie Jo's red herrings? Or another clue?

It was neither. When Ashley unwrapped the tissue she discovered a pendant — a gold-flecked marble attached to a thin golden chain. "It's beautiful!" she exclaimed. "Thanks, Auntie Jo! Thank you!"

She skipped into her bedroom, put on the pendant, and looked in the mirror. Sunlight was streaming through the window, and as she turned in the light, the marble changed colors. Bright yellow, pale amber, blood red. The flakes of gold sparkled one minute, shone the next. She placed her hand over the marble and was surprised at how warm it felt. She allowed herself to imagine that by removing it from its hiding place, she'd brought it to life.

As soon as her parents got home, Ashley showed them the pendant. Her father's reaction took her by surprise. "Good grief!" he said. "Jo's given you her goldstone!"

"You've seen this before, Dad? And it's really called a goldstone? It looks more like glass than stone." Ashley held the pendant up to the living room window. In the evening light the goldstone was almost transparent. Away from the light, it became opaque, the reddish-gold of autumn leaves. She liked that about the goldstone. There was more to it than first met the eye.

She spun the chain, and the goldstone cast honey-colored prisms. "It's a sun-catcher. See, Dad? But how do you know about a goldstone? I didn't think you were into jewelry."

"I don't know much about the jewelry part," he admitted, "but I know the goldstone's a family heirloom. I remember when Jo got it. I really wanted it for my marble collection, but no way. She wore it every-where. To school, to the beach, to parties, to the corner store. You look through the family albums. In every pic-ture of Jo, she's wearing that pendant. Guess she thought it was her good luck charm. Probably thought she'd be hit by lightning if she ever took it off."

"What about when she went to bed? Or in the shower?"

"Oh, Ashley, as if I'd know about that. But, yeah, she probably took it off in the shower. She wouldn't risk washing it down the drain. Where did you find it? That box looked so empty."

Ashley grinned. "It had a false bottom. And I, your brilliant daughter, discovered it."

"Trust Jo to turn a marble into a mystery. Everything she does is a scene out of a book."

"Have you thanked her yet?" Mom asked.

"Nope, but I'm going to. Right this very second."

Ashley hurried to her room and turned on the computer. "Thanks for the present," she muttered as she waited for the program to load. "What rhymes with *present*? *Meant, tent, dent* . . . Nope, too hard."

She switched to *gift* and thought awhile longer. *Sift*,

adrift. That should do it. She double clicked on NEW MESSAGE, typed BANKS ADRIFT on the subject line, and began to write.

Dear Auntie Jo,

I love my present. The goldstone is beautiful, even though it was hard to find. Dad said you used to wear it all the time for good luck. I hope you won't get bad luck now.

At first I thought your note "The future is coming" meant a present would come later in the mail. But now I've got the present. Instead of the future is coming, I could say "The present is here!" Both presents! Hey, a pun — I'd love your presense even better. (Did I spell that right?)

Love, Ashley

Two days later, Ashley received her aunt's reply. The subject was MOLDY BONES, and not the least bit difficult to figure out. MOLDY was a disguise for MOLD, which rhymed with GOLD. As for BONES? Simple! But the message hinted at another mystery.

Dear Ashley,

I'm glad you like the goldstone. It once belonged to my Aunt Karin, who lived in Revelstoke when she was your age. She died when I was a baby, but wanted me to have the goldstone. My grandparents gave it to me on my twelfth birthday, and now I'm passing it on to you.

I got the goldstone at a time when I needed something special. I wore it for years, never thinking it was more than a beautiful pendant and a link to the past. Later I learned

that the goldstone is a link to the future. Wear it at night,
and you'll see what lies ahead.
  Sweet dreams,
  Auntie Jo

Ashley laughed out loud. Was this her aunt's way
of saying the goldstone was magic, and that she could
dream the future? She must be working on a new book
about a fortune-teller.

She checked her watch, decided she had enough
time before supper, and wrote a reply to jgillespie@
aussiemail.com.au

Dear Auntie Jo,
  Here I was, thinking my life was boring, and I get a magic
stone for dreaming the future. I can't wait till tonight! How
does it work exactly? Do I ask a question and then the
answer appears in my dream? Do I say a certain year and
find out what's going to happen? As long as the answer's
not in rhyming code. I don't think I could figure THAT out
in my sleep!
  Honest. My life is SO boring!! Last year at school my
teacher Mr. Godfrey made us spend ten minutes every day
writing in our journals. We could write about anything
we wanted, and if we couldn't think of anything we had to
write, "I can't think of anything to write about." Mr.
Godfrey said the important thing was to keep writing.
Because sooner or later the action of moving your hand
across the page would bring up new ideas, and bursts of
creativity would flow from your mind through your hand

and out of your pen. Honest!! That's what he said! Like anybody believed it.

What do you think? Do you do that when you're writing? Maybe I'm wrong, maybe it works. But only for real writers like you, not for grade sixes. I hope my grade seven teacher has a better idea.

My boring life will get better pretty soon though 'cause Dad's taking me on his train run for my brithday. He had to get special premission and everything, even though he's the engineer. And in a few weeks it's Labour Day weekend and we're going camping at Glacier National Park. It's not far from here and it's a FABULOUS place and I love it. My best friend Erica's coming and so is Raven and his mom and his brothers. We're going to get two campsites together.

I'm so excited about dreaming on the goldstone!!! When I go back to school and we have to write about what we did during our summer holidays I'll have something great to say, for sure!!!

Mom just came in and said the BBQ was ready. Dad's wearing his BBQ apron and going goofy with the sauce so I hafta run. Bye!

Love, Ashley XX

That night Ashley went to bed without removing the pendant. How would it work? Would it have anything to do with her last thought before falling asleep? Better think of something nice to be on the safe side. Camping at Glacier, jumping off the dock at Williamson Lake, skiing down Spike run at Powder Springs, flying through pure powder . . .

Hours later, she woke up in a panic. Had she over-slept? What time was it? She threw back the covers and jumped out of bed. Then she remembered. It was summer. She didn't have to rush off to school. Talk about stupid.

As she was getting dressed, she noticed the gold-stone around her neck. Of course. She'd worn it to sleep. Had she dreamed the future? Not that she could remember.

She was brushing her hair when an image suddenly came to mind. It dissolved in an instant, like cotton candy — the moment you put it in your mouth, it vanishes. But there *had* been something there.

She closed her eyes and took several deep breaths to slow down her heartbeat. If she pretended she was asleep, she could maybe recapture the image and hold it long enough to make out a shape and form.

Something was coming. Not so much an image, but a feeling. It crept around the edges of her mind, an uneasy feeling of being pulled in two directions. Give, take. Go, stay. What was it?

She strained to remember, to bring back the smallest particle of the dream. Was there water? She remem-bered the sensation of swimming, so there must have been water. And something sharp. Something getting under her skin. Like a sliver of glass or a splinter. And something else . . .

Ohhh, it was maddening! Like looking through binoculars, seeing the hazy blur you *know* is a bird and trying to sharpen the focus before it flies away or dives beneath the surface of the water.

Ashley shook her head and opened her eyes. The image was gone. Nothing remained. Not a ripple, not even a flutter of wings.

7

The goldstone was back. Jonathan could feel its pulse.

It had to be the Ashley girl, this time. All he had to do was find her. And this time, she would not pass through him like air.

It took an enormous effort to shimmer into his body. First he had to remember it, to conjure up the Jonathan he once knew. Every detail — the black hair, the blue eyes, the calluses on his fingers and hands. His clothing had to be remembered, too. The scuffed toes of his boots. The worn leather gloves. The woolen cap. The blue mackinaw coat with its one missing button.

Once all the details were in place he had to summon the charge, the electrical impulse that would transform spirit into flesh and enable him to come and go as a real person. Until the shimmer wore off.

When that happened, he had to leave his body for a time and return to the ether world. There he drifted in the afterspace of fire and ice, the space left by the image of a flame the moment the candle has been extinguished. In that afterspace he rested and prepared himself for the next summoning charge.

He felt more charged than ever the day he shimmered into Revelstoke. He hardly recognized the place. How long had it been? A century. Ten thousand lifetimes. A heartbeat.

More than a heartbeat. Another pulse was beating. Leading him on. Drawing him closer and closer to the Ashley.

8

Every night Ashley dreamed on the goldstone.

Most dreams were like the first one, shadowy images that skirted around her consciousness and left her with an uneasy feeling. Some dreams were tantalizingly close, but impossible to grasp. Others revealed themselves in fragmented bits and pieces, usually when she least expected them to. There were no significant patterns, at least none that she could make out. And no common elements, except for the sliver.

Every few days she e-mailed her aunt, describing the dreams she could remember.

Did this happen to you? she wrote. *How does it work? Before I go to sleep I try to think about one specific thing, like what's going to happen when I'm thirteen or when I'm out of high school. But all that's a big blank. I usually dream little things, like the kind of pizza Mom's going to bring home tonight. I know it's going to be vegetarian with spinach and feta cheese even though I told her to get the one with pepperoni. And I knew that Dad and Raven would see a mountain bluebird when they went birding yesterday. I dreamed it in living color.*

See what I mean about my boring life? Birds I don't get to see and pizza I don't like. I have a very dreary future.

I told Mom and Dad but they didn't take it seriously. Mom laughed and said I was imagining things. Dad said I was just like you!!!

Erica thinks the goldstone's really cool. Especially since she got her swollen lip. What happened is I warned her not to take her usual route up town because if she did she'd be sorry. Erica said she'd do it as an experiment to see if I really could perdict the future. Then she phoned and told me she got knocked over from behind by this kid on roller-blades and had to go to emergency because her two front teeth cut into her lower lip when she fell and now she's got three stitches and a swollen lip. And I mean REALLY SWOLLEN!!! We read in a magazine about movie stars paying tons of money to get big lips. Well, Erica got hers for nothing. It doesn't last though. It's practically back to normal. Anyway, now she thinks I should set up a stand and start charging to tell fortunes. It'd be better than a lemonade stand. Especially since it's tourist season.

And she keeps bugging me to let her borrow the gold-stone. Talk about a pest!! Don't worry, I won't let her wear it because if anything happened to it I'd die. Raven says it's

*a big fluke, and if I let him wear it he'd prove it. He proba-
bly wants to dream on the goldstone to see if his mom and
dad get back together.*

*Only one week until my birthday on August 24th. (As
you know.) First a train trip with Dad and then Steph and
Erica are coming for pizza (MY choice for once and it's not
going to be feta cheese and spinach) and videos and a sleepover. I don't need a dream to know that's going to be GREAT!!!*

*Anyway, I better go to sleep now and dream what's going
to happen tomorrow!!!*

Love, Ashley

The goldstone was better than the psychic websites
she and Erica had found on the Internet. And it was
way better than the fortune-telling game Erica had got
one Christmas. Ashley had to admit it was fun, dreaming on the goldstone. Until the night she dreamed of
the boy buried in the snow.

She woke up, breathing hard, struggling to remember the details. *Look for the field marks.* That's what
Dad said whenever they went birding. Could she look
at the goldstone dreams the way she looked at birds?
What markings did they have that distinguished them
from her regular dreams? Snow wasn't unusual. She
lived in the Selkirk Mountains, famous for its heavy
snowfalls. She often dreamed of snow.

But the boy. Had she seen his face in the dream? Was
he someone she knew? Ohhh! She almost cried with
frustration. He was gone already, along with everything else in the dream. All that remained was the
feeling that something terrible was going to happen.

She looked at the time. It was two o'clock in the morning, and her birthday! In another three hours Mom would be waking her up for an early breakfast, then driving her to Field to meet Dad's train. She forced herself to stop worrying about the dream, and settled back down to sleep.

9

Jonathan sighed with despair.

Revelstoke was a confusion of paved roads and buildings and dykes along the river, of streetlights and colored lights and signs he couldn't read. The noise, the traffic, the people — he would never find the Ashley girl here.

Go into the mountains. Grandfather's voice whispered in his mind. *Follow the tracks . . .*

Everything had changed. Glacier House was gone. The tracks that had once crossed the summit of Rogers Pass were torn up, demolished, abandoned. The mountains no longer echoed with the whistle of steam. Trains no longer climbed over the pass. They rumbled beneath it, in the shelter of a tunnel cut deep inside the mountain.

And the trains! Jonathan had never seen such trains. They thundered over the steel rails, one mile long, their red engines pulling car after car after car. Blue and yellow and orange cars wove through the valleys like multicolored ribbons. Black cars, heaped with coal, slithered snake-like through the canyons.

And the noise! The trains clanked and squealed and roared and hissed. The walls of the tunnel shook with their passing. Even the mountains trembled.

Jonathan shimmered along the tracks, moving from the dark of the tunnel to the light of the valley. It was late summer, and already the leaves were changing color. Aspen, poplar, tamarack, birch . . . Gold, like the Ashley's hair.

Where would he find her? And when?

He brought back his dreams and searched for clues to tell him the time and the place.

And in the shadow of the Glacier, he watched and waited.

10

"All aboard!"

Ashley grinned up at her dad, waved good-bye to Mom, then grasped the handrails and climbed the steps of the diesel locomotive. She could tell one locomotive from another, and she knew that a bathtub gondola was a coal car, not some floating rubber toy. She knew that the mid-train helper units were called "robots," and she could spot a hopper car from a distance of twenty miles.

She often thought that when she grew up she'd like to be an engineer like her dad. For now, she was content to take a front-row seat on his mountain run, from Field on the Kicking Horse River to Revelstoke on the Columbia. The route would take them through the

Kicking Horse Canyon, past the town of Golden, and straight through the heart of Rogers Pass.

"Happy birthday, Ashley!" Bill, the conductor, welcomed her aboard. "Are you all set?"

"When do we start?" She had to shout to make herself heard. The deep rumble of the locomotives, coupled with the spit and hiss of pressurized air, made normal conversation impossible.

"Any minute now," he replied.

Up ahead, the signal changed to green. The dispatcher's voice came over the radio. "Are you ready to pull?"

"We have a clear signal," Dad said. He released the brakes and moved the throttle to Position One.

The locomotive inched forward. Ashley felt a tug as the slack was pulled out of the train. Eight thousand tons of freight began to move.

Few people were lucky enough to ride in the cab of a locomotive. When Raven heard that Ashley was going, he'd begged to be taken along, especially since it was his birthday, too. Dad said it couldn't be done, what with rules and regulations and so forth, but he promised to take Raven the following year. Ashley had to tell him all the details so he could add them to his collection of trivia.

She'd certainly tell him how she got to blow the whistle at the crossings — two long, a short, and a long. She'd also tell him about the noise. The squeal of wheels on the sharp turns, the screaming exhaust, the thundering roar of the engine — she should've brought ear plugs.

Farther along, a signal indicated they had to stop on a siding to wait for another train to pass. "Help yourself to a rail ale," Bill said.

Ashley opened a small fridge in the cab and took out the can of water he was referring to. "Want one?"

"Thanks," he said.

Dad took one too. "How do you like the ride so far?"

She mouthed the word *LOUD* as a mile-long grain train roared over the tracks. No wonder Dad liked a bit of peace and quiet when he came home.

When the last hopper car had rumbled by, the signal changed and the train rolled on. It wasn't a smooth ride. The roll of steel wheels shook Ashley from her toes to the top of her head. Even her fingertips quivered.

The train thundered over bridges and through tunnels, following the Kicking Horse River first through broad valleys, then through a deep and narrow canyon. White water rushed beneath the cliffs. The steel rails glimmered in the morning sun.

Soon they reached Golden, where the Kicking Horse River entered the Columbia. They passed a hundred-car coal train waiting on a siding, then began the long ascent into the Selkirk Mountains.

On the hillsides, the trembling aspens were already showing tinges of gold. The sight reminded Ashley of her goldstone. That dream last night, what had it revealed? A boy buried in the snow. And a sliver. The sliver that appeared in every dream, each time forcing itself deeper under her skin. And something else . . .

Suddenly she remembered. She'd dreamed of a purple glow in the mountains. She laughed to herself.

That meant nothing. Sunrise, sunset. Big deal.

Then another piece of the dream slipped into place. Words. There'd been words in the snow. Was it some kind of message?

"Wake up, Ashley! Grizzly!" Dad's voice jolted her back from her dreams. In the distance she could see a bear with two cubs, lumbering alongside the tracks.

Dad blasted the whistle and yelled out the open window, "Stay away from the tracks!" The bears turned and ran off. "Hope they get the message," he said to Ashley. "A lot of animals come for the grain that spills out of the hoppers, and, unfortunately, they don't always get out of the way." He took a long drink of rail ale. "Say good-bye to the sunlight. We're coming up to the Mount Macdonald Tunnel."

"The longest railway tunnel in the Western hemisphere," Ashley said. "Nine miles long to be concise. Is that the word? And it goes right under Mount Macdonald."

"Precise is the word," said Dad. "And you've been doing your homework. Or is that Raven's influence?"

"Yeah, well. Most of what he goes on about is forgettable. But sometimes he says stuff that's worth remembering."

"I'll have to tell him that."

"Da-ad! Don't you dare!"

They were now deep in the tunnel, and moving at a much slower speed. Dad got up and stretched, then bent down to a picnic basket sitting beside the fridge. "You ready for a snack? Mom's packed all sorts of goodies. Peanuts, raisins, chocolate chips — guess you'd call it rail mix — some cookies . . ."

"Stop!" Ashley cried suddenly.

"Wait, there's more. Sandwiches —"

"No, no! There's someone on the tracks! Stop the train!" She leaped up, grabbed his arm, and pulled him back to his seat.

He peered out the window, then turned and gave her a puzzled look. "There's nothing there. You see anything, Bill?"

The conductor looked up from his paperwork. "Nope."

"But there was," Ashley insisted. "It was a boy. I looked away for a second, and now he's gone. He was all lit up. He was standing on the tracks, staring straight at the train, and he didn't even try to get out of the way." She felt an unpleasant churning in her stomach. "I guess he got out of the way. We didn't run over him . . . did we?"

"Not a chance." Dad gave her shoulders a squeeze. "If there'd been anything there I would've seen it."

"But you weren't looking."

"True, but I know the tunnel was clear. You can see pretty far with these headlights. Nothing could have appeared that quick out of nowhere. You been drinking too much of that rail ale?" He gestured to the can of water and winked.

"No!" Ashley gave him a not-a-good-time-for-kidding glare. "I saw him."

"It's the lights and the shadows," Dad said. "They can play tricks on your eyes. Isn't that right, Bill? Happens to me, sometimes. Especially on the night runs."

Ashley nodded slowly, beginning to doubt herself. Could there really have been a boy on the tracks? It must have been a trick of the light. A shadow. A shimmer. Or maybe it was nothing more than a half-remembered dream.

11

Jonathan's power was growing. He could shimmer in and out of his body at will. He could make small things move. He could trip people, make them stumble and fall.

He could stir up a breeze. He could rustle leaves. He could melt ice. If he shimmered hard enough, he could bring down an avalanche.

But he still couldn't find the Ashley.

What dreams was she dreaming? Had she dreamed her future? Did she know it was linked to Jonathan's past?

Jonathan smiled. Maybe she would know him from her dreams. Maybe she would even know his name.

12

Every holiday weekend the Gillespies went camping with Raven's family, the McLeods. The tradition had started because of a comment made by Ashley's dad, the day he'd gone to the hospital to take his wife and newborn baby home. At the doorway he'd literally bumped into Raven's dad, who'd gone for the same reason. "We've got to stop meeting like this," Ian Gillespie joked, referring to the previous two days of hospital visits. And Marty McLeod had said, "Next time we'll make it a campsite."

Ashley and Raven didn't stand a chance. From that moment on they'd been thrust into Gillespie-McLeod get-togethers, outings, celebrations, and camping trips. They'd attended the same day care and kindergarten, gone to the same school, and, except for grade three, had always been in the same class. And Raven never let Ashley forget that although they shared the same birthday, he was three hours older.

When Raven was ten, his parents got divorced and his father moved to Golden. But the camping tradition had continued with his mother, and this Labour Day found them at a campground in Glacier National Park.

For the first time, Erica had come along. "I'm warning you, Raven," she said as she helped Ashley put up the girls' tent. "Don't you even think about pulling out these pegs." Both girls had noticed how intently Raven and his two younger brothers were watching the operation.

"Who, us?" Nine-year-old Jay grinned mischievously.

"Yes, you!" Erica made a threatening gesture, peg in hand. "I can see it now. You guys creeping out at night. And the tent falling on top of our heads."

"Thanks for the idea!" Corey, the six year old, beamed. "We never even thought of that, did we, Rave?"

"Nope. Not us."

"You girls almost finished?" Ashley's father said. "We're heading up the trail at ten hundred hours precisely. Five minutes from now."

Ashley hammered in the last peg and groaned. "Dad, you're on holidays. Not on railway time."

"No time like the present," he said.

"Time out!" Ashley countered.

"Time's a wastin'!"

"Come on, you two." Ashley's mother stepped in and put an end to the dueling clichés. "Round One to

Dad. Sorry, Ashley, but we've got to get going. It's a six-hour hike, there and back."

"Wait, wait!" Ashley grabbed Erica's arm and they ran to catch up to her dad. "How about time well spent?"

"I know one!" Corey piped up. "Quality time! We go to Golden every second weekend for quality time, don't we, Rave? Dad always says it's not quantity, it's the quality that counts."

"And you believe him?"

"Yeah . . . Don't you?"

Raven merely grunted. Then he gave Corey's baseball cap a tug and ran to join Ashley's dad.

The trail led them past many avalanche paths, reminding Ashley of her great-grandfather and the close call he'd once had with an avalanche. That made her think of her Great-Aunt Karin, who once lived in Revelstoke. She wondered if Karin had ever climbed this trail, and if she'd been wearing the goldstone like Ashley was now. The trail would have been different, of course. Everything would have been different. Back then, they didn't fire howitzers to trigger avalanches on purpose. And they didn't have a Parks Canada forecaster ready to close the highway so that the slides could roar harmlessly down the slopes. They didn't even have a highway back then.

"This way to the viewpoint," Dad said, leading them along a side trail. "Would've been somewhere around here that Major Rogers first viewed this pass, way back in 1881. Right down there — see where I'm pointing? That was the original route of the Canadian

Pacific Railway. And over there — hang on, that looks like a golden eagle! Quick, Raven, see it?"

As they continued up the main trail, Ashley's dad and Raven took turns spotting birds, while her mom stopped to record and photograph every wildflower they happened to see. Raven's mother strode on ahead, keeping pace with her two youngest sons. Ashley and Erica followed close behind, half-watching for marmots and pikas and bears, but more intent on discussing the upcoming first day back at school.

Late that afternoon, when everyone had finished lunch and hiked down the trail, they spent some time exploring the remains of a stone foundation. "This used to be Glacier House Hotel," Ashley's mom explained. "A very grand hotel. But it was closed down and abandoned, and after a few years it was officially wrecked. Such a shame. They shipped away anything worthwhile, then set fire to the rubbish. There's a model of Glacier House at the museum —"

Jay broke in with a loud sigh. "Why does everything have to be a lesson? I'm going to go back to the campsite and get the banana boats ready for tonight, OK, Mom? Race you, Corey! You, too, Raven! Go!" The boys sprinted off, followed by the adults, while the girls trailed behind.

"Jay, Raven, and Corey, short for Cormorant," Erica mused. "How come they all have bird names?"

"'Cause their mom's called Robin, I guess," said Ashley.

"Good thing you're not in their family. Hey, Ash?

You could've been called Finch or Chickadee. Or Bushtit."

Ashley laughed. "*You* could've been Sapsucker."

"Ooh! That sucks, Bushtit."

"You blue-rumped — ahh!" Ashley suddenly felt herself tripping over something. She cried out and landed hard on her knees. "Erica, you coot!"

"What? I didn't do anything!" She reached out a hand and helped Ashley to her feet. "You tripped on something."

"Like your big foot! What else? There's nothing sticking out on the trail."

"I didn't, honest! You tripped over your own big foot. You stumble-toed, clumsy-footed bushtit."

Ashley couldn't help but laugh. "Better than being a blue-rumped, brown-eyed junco like you." She leaned on Erica's shoulder and hobbled back to the campsite, keeping up the game of insults. Not so much for the fun of it, but to push away the feeling that *something* had tripped her on the trail.

13

"Once upon a time . . ."

No camping trip was complete without ghost stories, and over the years everyone had earned some sort of reputation. Jay's stories were the grossest. Corey's never made any sense. Raven's were the most boring, not only because his ghosts were masters of trivia, but because every story had to have a logical and scientific explanation. It was generally agreed that Ashley's dad had the best voice for telling ghost stories, so he was always persuaded to start.

"Once upon a time, when I was a teenager, I was out with my girlfriend, Kate . . ."

"It's supposed to be a ghost story," Jay complained. "Not your life story."

"It was a damp, foggy November night," Ashley's dad continued. "We were sitting in a car in Victoria, in Beacon Hill Park, in Lover's Lane. We were listening to the radio, and all of a sudden —" his voice became deeper, more chilling. "A news flash! A psychotic lunatic had escaped from an insane asylum! Listeners were warned that this lunatic was extremely danger-ous. How could he be recognized? By a blood-stained, razor-sharp hook where his hand used to be. Before it got chopped off. With an ax."

Ashley whispered, "So they called it an ax-ident."

"Ooh, death by puns," Dad groaned. "Talk about killing a mood. Anyhow, my girlfriend, Kate, who eventually became Ashley's mother, she started to worry. She wanted to go home in case the lunatic was prowling around in the park. I told her there was nothing to be afraid of, the insane asylum was miles from where we were. But you know Kate. Even way back then, nag nag nag. She insisted. I got a bit annoyed, backed up in a hurry, screeched out of the park. And drove her home.

"We both got out my side — we were sitting so close, you see — and I walked her to the door and kissed her goodnight. And as I was walking back to the car I saw something that made my blood run cold." His voice dropped to a shivery whisper. "There, on the passenger side, stuck in the handle of the door — was the hook!

"And to this very day, on damp, foggy November nights, that very same lunatic prowls Lover's Lane. And if you're there on a damp, foggy November night, if you're there and listening verrry, verrry hard, you can hear a ghostly voice saying, 'Briiing baaack my hoook . . .'"

There was a long silence. The campfire popped and sputtered. Then Corey exclaimed, "That's a cool story! But it isn't true, is it?"

Ashley's mom nodded. "Absolutely. Except for the nag part."

"I've got a ghost story," Jay said. "There's this guy, right? And they're going to a party, him and his girl-friend —"

"Eughhh!" Corey pulled a face. "Not another girl-friend story! Tell a *ghost* story."

"OK, here's another one. This kid had to go to the store to get some liver, right? But he met a bunch of his friends and they talked him into spending the money on ice cream cones. So then he doesn't have any money left for the liver. So he goes to the graveyard and digs up a grave and finds this body, right? So he brings home the liver and everybody eats it and says it's the best liver they ever tasted. But then at night when this kid's in bed . . ."

Ashley already knew the story about the ghost coming to get his liver. As Jay droned on, her mind wandered to the train tunnel, and the boy she had seen on the tracks. Who was he? Was he for real? If not, why would she have imagined something so strange?

A loud burst of laughter brought her back.

"Thank you, thank you," Jay was saying. "Hold the applause."

"That's definitely not true," said Corey.

"Yeah, it is. You know that stew you ate for supper? That Ashley's mom said was beef? Well, it was really liver. And guess whose it was? Go on, guess."

Corey whacked him on the arm. "I hate you, Jay."

"Remember that mean guy who used to live across the street? It's his liver."

"Mom, tell him to stop."

"He's teasing," his mother said. "Of course it wasn't anybody's liver. It was beef. Glorious, succulent, tender beef."

Jay persisted. "Chef Camponi Surprise, that's what Kate called it, remember? And that was the surprise! The liver!"

"Enough, enough," Ashley's dad said. "How about you, Ashley? Have you got a ghost story?"

"I saw a ghost on the train." She spoke hesitantly, half-afraid the others would laugh. "I mean, I was on the train and the ghost was on the tracks. In the tunnel. Remember, Dad? Only Dad didn't see him."

"What was he wearing?" Jay asked.

"Nothing."

"You mean he was bare naked?" Corey squealed.

"No, it was as if I could see right through him. He was just . . . light."

"Whoa, that's intense," said Raven. "Just, uh, light."

Ashley poked him in the ribs. "Quit making fun of me, you blue-bellied nose-picker."

"Yeah, Raven," Erica joined in. "Skinny-legged, zit-flecked nerd."

"Better than being a fluff-headed tattle-snipe like you."

"Enough!" Dad's booming voice surprised everyone into silence. "Let's get back to the ghosts. I figure this whole pass is riddled with ghosts. Especially in the early days of the railway, what with all the avalanches. My grandfather was involved in one, not far from here. But you all know that story."

"I don't," Corey said. "Tell us! But wait till I get another banana boat. Anybody else want one? They're the best, 'cause me and Jay made them."

They used a poker to pull the banana boats out of the fire, then opened the aluminum foil. Inside was a gooey mess of melted marshmallows, chocolate chips, peanuts, and banana, hot and delicious.

"Now you can tell the story," Corey said, licking chocolate off his spoon. "Make it scary, but no liver."

"My grandad was the roadmaster for the Canadian Pacific Railway," Ashley's dad began, "and one night a huge avalanche came down Cheops Mountain, right at the summit of Rogers Pass. It buried the tracks some twenty feet deep. So Grandad calls out his crew and off they go, in blizzard conditions, to clear the tracks so the trains can go through. Around about midnight, Grandad leaves the site, hikes down the line to the phone, and when he gets back, everybody's gone. Another avalanche had come down, this time from Avalanche Mountain, and buried everything. Sixty-two men died."

"And your grandad was saved because somebody phoned him?" Corey said. "Who was it? Who was on the phone?"

Raven rolled his eyes. "No, genius, *he* was the one who phoned. Probably to let the dispatcher know when the trains could start running again. He was the roadmaster, so he was responsible."

"He was lucky."

"Sure was," Ashley's dad went on. "And a fellow called Bill LaChance —"

"That's French for lucky," Erica said.

"You're right. And it's true, he was one lucky man. Grandad found him in the snow, still alive, and rescued him. He was the only survivor. You can hear his story at the Rogers Pass Centre. That's on the schedule for tomorrow."

"Speaking of which," said Ashley's mom, "I think it's time for bed."

"Don't forget the peg-pulling, Ashley!" Jay grinned. "As soon as you and Erica are aslee-eep . . ."

Raven stirred the coals with the poker and doused the fire while the others cleaned up the campsite, making sure that any food was safely out of the way of bears. "I bet there's a storm tonight," Raven said. "You guys feel it? It's really warm and close."

"A storm?" Corey's small face scrunched up with worry. "With lightning?"

"You don't have to be scared of lightning," Raven said. "It's only an electrical spark caused by electrons moving from one place to another. They move so fast they make the air around them glow. That's what makes a lightning flash."

"Nobody cares," Jay said. "Nobody's listening."

Raven was on a roll. "A streak of lightning is actually the path that the electrons follow as they blast their way through the air."

"He does that," Jay explained to Erica. "Acts like he knows everything even though he doesn't."

"Tell me about it," Erica said. "I've been in his class for six years, remember."

"Would you believe there's about eighteen hundred thunderstorms happening around the world every minute? And every *second* there's one hundred lightning bolts striking the earth."

Corey looked nervous. "What if we get hit by lightning?"

"Then you're bacon," said Jay. "Sizzled. Zapped. Fried. And then we eat your liver. It's called Corey Surprise Stew."

"Mo-om . . ."

"A lightning path branches out in different directions —"

"Enough, Raven," his mother said.

"Like the branches of a tree. And when —"

"OK, Professor," Ashley's dad broke in. "The fire's out. Time to call it a day."

Ashley was half-asleep when a sliver of dream came back. Strange how she thought of it that way, a sliver of dream. Like the sliver *in* her dream. Needle-sharp. Probing. Searching for something, for one particular nerve that would carry a connection to the brain. As if there was something she should know. Something she should be able to figure out.

In the dream she was moving across a snowfield, following someone. No . . . Someone was following *her*. She tried to concentrate, to bring the image in closer. But just when she thought she had a clear picture, a streak of lightning ripped the sky and lit up the inside of the tent.

"Ashley?" Erica whispered. "Are you awake?"

An echo of thunder bounced forcefully off the mountains. Then another bolt of lightning scrawled a path across the sky.

Erica shook Ashley's arm. "Ashley, wake up! Wake up!"

"Ten seconds," Ashley said, as another rumble of thunder shook the earth. "The storm's two miles away."

"I don't care — huh? How do you figure that?"

"When you first see the lightning, you count the seconds until you hear the thunder. Then divide by five. That tells you how far away the storm is. Raven told me."

"Oh, no! There's another one!" Erica dove into her sleeping bag and held the pillow to her ears.

The storm was directly overhead. Rain began to fall, so hard and fast it seemed it would tear through the tent.

Erica poked her head out from under the pillow. "Is this tent waterproof?"

"We'll soon find out," said Ashley. She could hear Corey wailing in the adjoining campsite. "What if we're hit by lightning! Mo-om! I don't wanna get fried!"

The next crack of thunder sounded like a thousand drums beating in her head.

"Oh, God! I can't stand it!" Erica grabbed Ashley's arm with such force her battered fingernails dug into the skin.

"Ouch!" Ashley cried and yanked her arm away. "You're not scared, are you? It's just a storm. At least you won't have to worry about the boys skulking around and collapsing our tent."

"You can get hit by lightning, you know. Then you die."

"You're not going to die, Erica. Not tonight. Unless I kill you. I'll never get back to sleep now. My arm hurts too much."

"I'm sorry, OK? Look . . . Don't tell anybody."

"What? That you were scared witless? Of course I won't tell. I'm your best friend. I've got the scars to prove it."

"Count the seconds and divide by five. I'll have to remember that."

"Hear the thunder now? It's way farther away. And the rain's stopped." Ashley paused for a moment. "Know what? I was scared, too. I felt like running into Mom and Dad's tent."

"Really? You never act like you're scared about anything. I have to tell you, this is so cool being out here, especially now that the storm's over. Raven was right, wasn't he? Whoa! That was some storm . . . So you go camping with Raven every single holiday?"

"Just in the summer. Ever since I was born."

"You're so lucky."

"I know. I love camping."

"Not that!" Erica lowered her voice to a whisper.

"I mean lucky to go camping with Raven."

Ashley frowned. That was lucky?

"Do you like him?" Erica asked.

"Of course! He's like my brother."

"No, I mean *really* like him."

"I don't know! I never even thought about it."

"I do. I'm crazy about him. If we're not in the same class this year, I'll die."

"I hope we're all in the same class," Ashley said. "And I hope we get Mrs. Irvine."

"Hey, Ash? I just thought of something. You know today, when your mom was doing all the wildflower stuff and your dad was naming every bird and mountain and Raven was saying all that stuff about lightning . . ."

"Yeah, so?" Ashley yawned.

"And you know how you and Raven were born in the same hospital at the same time — well, almost — did you ever think they might have switched babies? By mistake, I mean."

Ashley snorted with laughter. "You're crazy!"

"I know. I'm in love. But admit it, Ash. Raven is way more like your parents than you are."

"Come off it!"

"One more thing, and then I'm going to sleep. And this sounds really weird so don't laugh. But today at the ruins, at the Glacier House place, did you see that kid? He was lurking around the stone walls. He looked right through me, like I was some kind of, I don't know, weed or something, but he sure looked interested in you. I even saw him smile at you. But your back was turned so I guess you didn't see him. Did you?"

There was a long silence.

"Hey, Ash, are you asleep? Am I talking to myself?"

"No," Ashley whispered. She couldn't say more because another sliver of dream had fallen into place, a sliver that pierced so deep it made her tremble. It was the image of a boy standing in the shadows, his face half-lit by an eerie glow. He was watching and waiting. And somehow she knew he was watching and waiting for her.

Later she awoke with still another piece of remembered dream. This time it was a path. Not sharp and jagged like the path made by lightning, but long and straight and smooth, like the path made by an avalanche.

14

Where had all the people come from?

Jonathan watched in horror as they spilled into his mountains and clamored along the trails. They shout-ed and yelled, whistled, laughed, and sang. They banged rocks together. They shook clusters of bells.

Go away! Jonathan wanted to scream. Go back to your towns!

The people scared away the wildlife. They destroyed the silence. They trampled on the memory of his grandfather.

They angered the spirits, who split the sky with ferocious bolts of lightning.

But the lightning could not drive the people away.

Even the Ashley girl stayed.

Jonathan knew her the instant he saw her, and not only because she was wearing the goldstone. He was standing in the ruins of Glacier House when she walked by, her fair hair shining in the light, the way he'd seen it in his dream.

He was sorry she was so noisy, although she wasn't as loud as her companions. Shouts, squeals, high-pitched laughter — weren't they ever still? They tossed words back and forth as if they were afraid of silence. As if they were afraid that one small space of quiet would swallow them up and muffle their voices forever.

And the boy with the brown hair, he was the worst. He *never* stopped talking. Fortunately he ran on ahead with the two younger boys. The adults followed and left the girls to themselves.

Good. He needed the Ashley alone. If he could get rid of the other girl . . .

He shimmered out of his body so he couldn't be seen, then stuck out a foot. The Ashley would trip and fall and the dark-haired girl would go running for help.

It didn't work as planned. It didn't even stop the talking.

He would have to wait awhile longer. Watch and wait. Until he could get her alone.

All at once he remembered. It wasn't the time. Not now, not at the end of summer. In his dreams of the Ashley, there had always been snow.

15

On the weekends Raven didn't go to Golden, and if Ashley's dad's work schedule allowed it, the two often did something together. "It's a guy thing," Raven liked to say when Ashley complained about being left out. Their outings, from birding to backcountry skiing, had become as much of a tradition as the holiday camping trips.

On this particular Saturday, two weeks after Labour Day, they were birding in Glacier National Park. Raven was glad to be out and away from his brothers, especially since they couldn't stop talking about the previous weekend, the one they'd spent at their dad's.

His mom was just as bad, wanting to know everything. And Jay and Corey were only too happy to fill in the details.

Not that it wasn't on Raven's mind. He just didn't want to talk about it. Except, maybe, to Ashley's dad, Ian.

But birding was a quiet activity. You couldn't make a lot of noise or you'd scare away the birds. And if you did get into a conversation, you were always being interrupted. A sudden flash of color, a beating of wings, a sharp chirp, a rapid warble — up went the binoculars, out came the notebooks, and all talk switched to field marks and species. So instead of telling Ian about the disastrous weekend, Raven spotted birds and recorded them in his notebook. Rosy finch. Common raven. White-tailed ptarmigan . . .

He was barely concentrating. The whole time, even when they came to a small alpine lake and stopped for lunch, he was imagining the tortures he'd like to inflict on his father, the chestnut-bearded louse. And on the common, tan-throated, melon-breasted shrike he was seeing. Misty. Even her name disgusted him. How could his father take up with someone called *Misty*? And how dare he take Raven aside at the end of the weekend and say, "I want you to like her. I want you to become great friends. OK, buddy? I'm counting on you."

Count me out, Raven thought angrily. *Buddy.*

"Want another sandwich?" Ian's voice broke into his thoughts.

When Raven shook his head with a mumbled, "No, thanks," Ian said, "You want to tell me what's bothering you? I've never known you to be so quiet. Not just voice quiet, but attention quiet. If you follow me."

Raven felt a lump rise in his throat. Ian knew him so well. Why couldn't he have *him* for a father? "Yeah, well . . . Last weekend in Golden. It wasn't just us and Dad. This other person — hey." He stopped abruptly, his attention drawn to a movement across the lake. It was a welcome distraction. Raven had never been one to express his feelings, and he'd no sooner started to confide in Ian than he was regretting it. Fortunately, the distraction solved the problem of what to say next.

"Is it a bird?" Ian reached for his binoculars.

"No, a kid. Weird. He's dressed like it was winter. Boots, gloves, the whole bit." He stood up and waved, shouting, "Hey, kid!"

There was no response.

"Blue coat? Woolen cap pulled over his ears?"

"Yeah! You see him?" Raven looked through his own binoculars. "Rats. Now I don't see him at all."

"Looks like he's gone." Ian scanned the far shore of the lake, then lowered his binoculars. "Want to hike to the other side, see if he's got a camp set up? We can take a look after lunch."

They found no trace of the boy, not even the remains of a campfire. But they did spot one of the last of the season's golden-crowned sparrows, which made Ian's day.

As they were making their way back down, Ian picked up the thread of their earlier conversation. "You were telling me about last weekend. Something happen at your dad's?"

"Nah . . . nothing much," Raven mumbled. What

was the point of talking about it? Talking wouldn't change things. It would just make him all the more angry. But it was nice of Ian to ask.

They hiked for a while in silence, then Ian said, "Not much longer till ski season. We'll have to come touring up here again. What do you think? Nice gentle slopes by the lake. Good backcountry territory for us old pros, eh?"

Raven grinned. For the first time in a week he had something to look forward to.

As for that kid disappearing? There was a rational explanation. He was a hiker, dressed warmly in case of snow at higher elevations. He was a loner, didn't want to chat, took off when he saw them coming. It had taken them long enough to get around the lake. The kid had plenty of time and plenty of places to hide. And why not? The mood Raven had been in that morning, he would have done the very same thing.

16

Where was the Ashley?

Jonathan recognized the boy and the man. But where was the Ashley girl? Why wasn't she with them?

As soon as Jonathan saw them start up the trail he'd kept watch, half-expecting the Ashley to follow. Later, at the lake, he'd hoped that she would join them. But she hadn't.

The man and the boy weren't as noisy as the last time he'd seen them. This time they were watching for birds and had to be quiet.

Jonathan understood. He and Grandfather had spent long hours in the mountains watching the birds, especially in the summer. It was fall now and most of the birds were migrating. Soon there would be snow.

Jonathan longed for the snow, for the dazzling whiteness of the high alpine fields. And the quiet! The snow would muffle sounds and give silence back to the mountains.

He left the boy and the man to the birds and the lake and shimmered to the summit of the pass.

Some things had not changed. Standing at the summit, Jonathan could still gaze down into the gorge. Above him, and all around, the glaciers still gleamed in the sunlight. The largest of all, the Great Glacier, looked smaller than before, as if it were retreating into the mountains. But it still showed him the way home. And to Grandfather's place, deep beneath the ice.

Part of the abandoned railway bed still remained at the summit. So did the ruins of the snowshed that was smashed to splinters the night of the avalanche.

The tunnel was gone, the tunnel formed when the plow had sliced an opening in the snow. Jonathan remembered taking a shovel into the tunnel that night. He remembered digging to clear the tracks. He remembered the walls closing in.

He remembered laughing. One of the men on the crew had lit a cigarette, then told a joke. Jonathan remembered the acrid smell of the tobacco and the glow of the kerosene torch. He remembered the feel of the laughter, although he couldn't remember the joke. Maybe he hadn't understood it but had laughed anyway. To be like the others. To be liked by the others. Young men who might have become his friends.

Where were they now? Did they shimmer along the

tracks, watching and waiting? Did they have promises to keep?

The wind grew chill. Leaves fell from the trembling aspens. The people invading the mountains began to go away.

Jonathan found a measure of silence along the old railway bed. And it was there, when the first flakes of snow began to fall, that he finally came face to face with the Ashley.

17

"What you're standing on now," the guide was saying, "is the, um, site of the abandoned railway tracks."

Raven caught Ashley's eye and mouthed one word. *Borrr-ing.*

Ashley nodded in agreement. It didn't help that she knew the story inside out.

She wished Raven would interrupt with a choice fact or two. She wished Erica would stop chewing her nails and faint. She wished *she* had the knack of fainting. Or a talent for something.

"Here, right where you're standing, is where the, um, avalanche came down and killed fifty-eight men. It was the worst disaster in the history of the Canadian Pacific Railway."

"Sixty-two." Raven corrected the guide, then continued in spite of a warning glance from his teacher. "Fifty-eight bodies were found right after the slide, but four more were found, um, a few days later."

"Raven . . ." Mrs. Irvine glared.

"Well, I can't help it!" Raven retorted. "They should get the facts right." He flashed a look at Ashley, who barely managed to hold back a giggle.

The guide thanked Raven for the information and led the class to the remains of the demolished snowshed. That part of the tour over and done with, she herded the group along the abandoned railway trail and back to the Rogers Pass Centre.

Ashley lingered behind. This was not a place for noisy groups, but for quiet reflection. Right here, in this very spot, people had lost their lives. Her very own great-grandfather . . .

Unexpectedly, she felt a stirring of air, although the leaves remained motionless.

Snow was starting to fall. She shivered and began to feel uneasy. Ashley was about to leave when she heard the snap of a twig. A bear? It was late in the season for bears, but still . . . She turned around slowly and saw a boy standing on the trail.

"Oh, hi!" She smiled, relieved. She didn't know where he had come from. The tour bus, maybe? If so, he was in trouble. The bus had already left the parking lot. He didn't look like a tourist, though. Or a hiker. He had no camera, no backpack, nothing. And his clothes! His coat and his overalls looked like the sort of thing you'd find in an old-fashioned thrift shop. And they were way too big, as if he was shrinking inside.

The boy was standing half in light, half in shadow, gazing at something in his hand. A soft glow lit up his pale face.

He looked oddly familiar. And suddenly Ashley knew why. Her heart raced and a tingling sensation crept along the back of her neck. She reached up to her throat and grasped the goldstone. "You — you were in the train tunnel. And in my dream."

The boy moved his lips. She heard a low thrumming sound, muffled by the falling snow.

"What? What are you saying?"

The boy smiled. And vanished.

Ashley stood frozen, her thoughts whirling like snowflakes in a blizzard. Who was he? Why couldn't she hear him? Where did he come from? Where did he *go*? She gulped down a mouthful of cold air, shook herself to clear her head, and ran back to the Centre.

She found her class gathered around a large model showing the aftermath of the Rogers Pass avalanche. As soon as the guide finished her talk and moved everyone off to another display, Ashley motioned for her friends to stay behind. In a hushed and hurried voice, she told them what she'd seen.

"He what?" Erica said.

"He vanished! That's what I'm trying to tell you!"

"Cool!"

"How did he vanish?" Raven wanted to know. From Ashley's description the boy sounded identical to the one he'd seen across the lake, so he couldn't tease her about hallucinating. But *vanished*? He snapped his fingers. "Did he disappear like that? One minute here, the next minute gone? Or was it a slow, gradual fading out? Or maybe you just *think* he vanished."

"It's almost Halloween," Erica pointed out. "Could be you're seeing things."

"Maybe he only turned the corner and walked out of sight," Raven continued. "It's snowing hard, Ashley. You probably wiped your eyes and he went back to the tour bus or something."

"The bus was gone already. Oh, I don't know." Let Raven find a rational explanation. She preferred the mystery.

That night, she e-mailed Auntie Jo about the vanishing boy. She typed MAN-FISHING TOY on the subject line, made the server connection, and sent the message.

She thought again about Raven finding a rational explanation. He could try all he liked. She definitely preferred the mystery, as long as it didn't come any closer. But why would it? She'd dreamed the boy and now she'd seen him. End of story.

Yet something about the boy, the way he smiled, made her think it was only the beginning.

18

"Ashley, the Ashley . . ." The name sounded like a whisper, a lullaby Jonathan remembered from a long ago time. "Hush, hush little baby . . ."

Had the mother sung the lullaby? *Hush little baby, don't say a word. Mama's gonna buy you a mockingbird . . .* Was that how it went?

She hadn't bought him a mockingbird. Or a hummingbird. Not even a blackbird.

There had been a black bird in his dreams, he remembered. A raven. But the raven was a mystery.

The Ashley wasn't a mystery, now that he'd found her. The dreams had told him she'd have the goldstone, and she did. He'd seen her reach for it. He'd seen the way it shone between her fingers, half-hidden beneath her jacket. A red jacket with bright yellow trim. Columbine colors. Like in the dreams.

The dreams had also told him the raven would point the way. But how?

Patience, my son. You've waited this long.
But it's so close!
Patience . . .
But, Grandfather, couldn't I follow her home? Couldn't I take the goldstone while she's asleep? She wouldn't know.
Remember the dream, my son. Is it the time? Is it the place?
I made a promise, and now it's so close!
Patience . . .

Jonathan watched through the falling snow as the Ashley got on the yellow bus with the others. He watched the bus turn onto the highway and head for the town.

He would go to the town and wait for the bus. He would watch her get off. He would follow her home.

The goldstone was too close for patience. The time was right. The waiting was over.

19

Seated at her computer on the other side of the world, Jo read Ashley's e-mail with growing alarm. Not so much because of the encounter it described, but because of the long-forgotten memory it triggered.

It was the summer of 1962. Jo had just graduated from high school and had gone on a family trip to Banff via the new Rogers Pass Highway. On the way, they had stopped at the summit to see the site where the avalanche had buried her grandfather's crew.

They took several pictures and were on their way back to the car when Jo saw a strange flickering light accompanied by a humming sound. She thought it was an insect and jumped back as if she'd been bitten.

A few moments later she looked over her shoulder

and was amazed to see the light again, transforming into the shape of a person. She stared, in stunned disbelief, as the light-person swept the air with its arm as if calling her back. Then it had disappeared. Just like Ashley's vanishing boy.

Jo reread the e-mail, searching for more connections.

The weird thing is, the boy looked exactly the way he looked in my dream! He had black hair down to his shoulders and the darkest blue eyes I've ever seen. Not like mine. (Dad calls them blue heron eyes because they're sort of grayish-blue.) Anyway, this boy's eyes were big and wide apart with long black lashes that Erica would die for. He smiled and looked happy to see me like he KNEW me. But there was something else in his eyes that made me kind of nervous. Like he was TOO happy, if you know what I mean. OK, if you want the truth he was really good-looking but he gave me the creeps. It's too bad Erica wasn't there because she would have said something to make him back off. Not me. Whenever I get nervous I just calm up! Anyway, he started talking but I couldn't hear what he said. Even though he was SO CLOSE and I couldn't lip read . . .

"Oh, no," Jo gasped. "It can't be."

Outside in her garden the kookaburras were flying in for their daily frolic in the birdbath and creating their usual ruckus. Jo paid no attention. All she could think about was a throbbing hum, not from the encounter she'd had on the summit, but later when she'd fallen asleep in the car. She'd forgotten about that. And until this very moment she'd forgotten the dream she'd had. Now it came back. The light, the smile, the eyes — it was the same boy. And in Jo's dream he was speaking. She couldn't hear the words, only that humming vibration, and she couldn't tell who he was speaking to. But she could read his lips. *Give me the goldstone. I've come to take it back.*

And then another dream flashed into her mind. The dream she'd had the night before she sent the gold-stone to Ashley. She couldn't remember the details but she certainly recalled crying out in the night and waking up in a cold sweat. She'd put it down to some sort of panic attack caused by too many deadlines. Not by a dream. Until now.

Jo got up from the computer and went outside, her stomach sick with anxiety. What have I done? she asked herself. I gave Ashley the goldstone. I told her about dreaming the future. What should I tell her now?

There was only one thing to do. She had to see Ashley in person. And for some reason she felt she had to get her away from the snow.

But when? She had deadlines, tours, and commit-ments straight through until February. After that, she was free.

In the meantime, she would write to Ashley and suggest, in a light-handed way, that maybe she should stop wearing the goldstone to sleep. She would also assure her there was nothing whatsoever to worry about. After all, a dream was just a dream.

20

"Entrez, entrez! Come in and ask Madame a question. Madame Citrona knows all."

"Oh, Erica!" Ashley giggled as she stepped into the dimly lit alcove adjoining the school library. The only light source was an electric heater plugged into the wall. A red bulb glowed behind a fake pile of logs, and thin strips of foil crackled and flickered with the help of a built-in fan. It was highly artificial, but it did give the illusion of a campfire.

The alcove was draped with a silky blue-and-white fabric that flowed across the walls and ceiling and separated the area from the rest of the library. It was supposed to look like a night sky with Milky Way swirls.

"*Asseyez-vous!* Madame Citrona will answer all your questions."

Ashley sat as directed. The small, round table was covered with a brocade cloth woven in red, blue, and gold. It was an obvious leftover, since Erica was dressed in the same brocade. Another leftover scrap appeared in the scarf that held back her hair. Heavy makeup, silver hoop earrings, and seven jangling bracelets completed the effect. Ashley wasn't sure about the nose stud or the black fingernail polish.

"Madame Citrona waits." Erica flashed her dark eyes, then lowered her heavily accented voice and placed her hands on the glass ball. "Don't be afraid. *Demandez!* Ask Madame a question. She will read the answer that lies inside her crystal ball. But first you must cross her palm with silver. One question for a dime. Three for a quarter." She held out her hand.

Ashley placed a dime in the outstretched hand. "Will I be rich and famous and live happily ever after?"

Erica stared into the crystal ball. "*Attendez* . . . The vision is not clear. Wait, wait . . . Ahh, yes. But oh, no, this is not good. Madame Citrona sees only *noir*. So much black! So much darkness! Like *le corbeau*, the raven that hovers over your house. Madame Citrona thinks you must speak to the raven. You must tell him —"

"You goof!" Ashley laughed. "You're supposed to answer my question!"

"Come on, Ash!" Erica said, reverting to her normal voice. "Is it too much to ask your best, best, best, best friend? Just tell Raven I like him. And find out if he likes me. Puh-leeze! He's over at your house all the time. He even lives on your street! God, you're lucky. So tell him, OK?"

"All right! Stop groveling."

"*Merci, merci*, I owe you a thousand favors. So how did I do? Did I sound like a Madame Citrona?"

"You mean like a lemon?"

"No, seriously. Do I look all right? Did I sound all right? What about the French? Tell me the truth. And if you don't say something nice I'll trade places and you'll have to be the fortune teller and I'll sell the cotton candy. Ohhh, maybe I *should* do something different. When is this stupid fair?"

"You know it's tonight. And anyway, you were perfect. Except you never did answer my question. And except for the lipstick on your tooth."

"Euugh, I hate that! Which tooth?"

"That crooked one at the front." Ashley pointed to the tooth and watched as Erica rubbed off the red smear. "You could have added more raven stuff."

"I'm not doing ravens for everybody, *duhh*. Just for you. Everybody else gets boring stuff. Like, you will wake up tomorrow and go to school. It's supposed to be yes/no answers, but sometimes I elaborate. See, if someone asks, 'Will I make a lot of money in the future?' I say, 'No, you will go to school and fail your math test.' Stuff like that. You want to know how I do it?" She went on to explain while removing her costume. "I've got a bunch of yes cards and no cards in my lap. I shuffle them, then draw a card each time someone asks a question. Cool, eh? I do it secretly so no one'll know."

"What about my question? Will I be rich and famous and live happily ever after?"

"That's actually three questions. So Madame Citrona says you shouldn't get an answer unless you pay a quarter. But just this once she'll give you a deal. The answer is yes."

"That's a relief."

"But only if you find out if Raven likes me." She picked up her backpack, unplugged the heater, and followed Ashley out of the library.

As they walked down the hall, they paused to glance inside the various classrooms where teachers, parents, and kids were busily setting up for the Fall Fair. "Is Raven coming tonight?" Erica asked.

"Probably. Why don't you ask him yourself?"

"Jeez, Ash. I don't want to be obvious."

Outside, a cold November wind was blowing the snow that had fallen the day before, and from the appearance of the sky, more snow was on its way.

"So you really think my costume's perfect?" Erica said. "So you'll let me wear the goldstone to make it even more perfect?"

"Erica, you've already asked and I said no."

"Oh, come on, Ash! Please? I know it's really special but I'd guard it with my life."

"Nope!"

"I'll give you ten dollars. Twenty? A hundred?"

"NO! So forget it."

"If it was mine I'd let *you* wear it."

"Erica, stop!"

"Oh, all right." She pouted for a moment, then carried on. "Do you think I should use more French? I think I should 'cause it sounds way more fortune-tellerish. And another thing . . ."

Ashley half-listened as they walked down the wide, tree-lined street. She found herself wishing she could have been the fortune teller. But her coloring made her look more like a Viking than a gypsy, and she knew she'd clam up the minute someone asked her a tricky question. Plus, if anyone started laughing, she'd be too mortified to carry on. Unlike Erica.

Oh, well. Selling cotton candy wasn't bad, as long as she remembered her hairband. Last year was a disaster. Pink cotton candy had matted throughout her hair, the shirt she'd worn was a spun-sugar nightmare, and her hands and arms had felt sticky for days. Yuck! What was she doing? Why hadn't she volunteered at the white elephant booth? Or at the bake sale with Mom?

"I'll never forgive you for not letting me wear your necklace. Unless you tell Raven I like him."

"Hmm?" said Ashley.

"Aren't you even listening? Tell him I like him and see what he says! Jeez, Ash, pay attention!" Erica rolled her eyes and waved as she turned down her street. "See you at 5:30. And don't be late 'cause you have to help me with my makeup."

"Why don't you ask Raven?" Ashley called after her. "He's good at painting."

"Very funny, Ash. See you later."

What's so special about Raven? Ashley wondered. She'd tell him, if the time was right, but she knew what he'd probably say. *Eughhh! You've got to be kidding!* Naturally she would keep that part to herself.

She reached the end of the next block and turned the corner. As she was coming up to Raven's house she saw him run down the front steps and into the yard. She was just thinking, now would be a good time to tell him, when the shouting started.

"Forget it! I'm not going!" Raven glowered at the car parked in the driveway, and as he continued to shout, the trunk popped open. Jay and Corey came running outside, threw in their backpacks and overnight bags, and climbed into the backseat.

"You better get in, Raven!" Jay said.

"I told you already! Forget it!"

As Ashley stood watching, a young woman got out of the driver's seat and walked over to Raven. "We've got to get going," she said pleasantly. "Your dad's got hockey tickets for tonight's game and I know you don't want to miss it."

"*You* know?" Raven gave her a scathing look. "You don't know the first thing about me. And you can tell Dad I got better things to do this weekend."

Corey leaned out the window. "Come on, Rave. Please! Dad's got videos and the best food. He even said."

"It's just bribery, you little jerk."

"Raven —"

"Forget it!" He brushed past the woman's outstretched hand and stomped into the house.

At that point, Jay leaned out the window and yelled, "Hey, Ashley! Tell Raven he's gonna get it when Dad finds out. And Mom's gonna be really ticked off." He smiled and waved as the car drove off.

Ashley hesitated, wondering whether she should go straight home or stay for a minute and talk to Raven.

"Take off!" he shouted when she knocked on the door. "I'm not going, for the millionth time!"

"It's me, Ashley. They've gone already."

"Oh. Well, come in if you want."

She went inside and found him glaring at the weather channel. "You're not going to your dad's this weekend?"

"You were there. Figure it out."

"How come?"

"Because I hate that woman. And I hate my dad. He can't even come to get us anymore. He has to send her. Like I want to sit in *her* car for over an hour."

"She looks nice."

"A lot you know."

"Well . . . I better get going. You coming to the Fall Fair?"

"I doubt it. Maybe."

"Jay said your mom's going to be mad. Was she planning to go away this weekend or something?"

"Nahh, she won't care. Jay doesn't know what he's talking about. Anyway, why shouldn't I stay home if I want to? Dad can take his quality time and shove it."

"See you later, then."

"Wait a sec." He stopped her as she was going out

the door. "Is your dad working this weekend?"

"Not on Sunday. We're going skiing at Powder Springs."

"Can I come?"

"Sure, I guess."

"Great!" He gave her a big grin.

Ashley walked away feeling a bit annoyed with herself. Sunday was supposed to be her day with Dad. Why did she say Raven could come? He was at her place so much, why didn't he just move in? She couldn't help but smile at that scenario. Erica would go out of her mind.

"Hi, honey," Mom said when Ashley got home. "Have a good day? All set for the fair? Do you want a ride? I'm at the bake stand so I've got to be there at quarter to six."

"Nope, I'm walking with Erica." She opened the cookie tin, took the last two chocolate chip cookies, found the shopping list hidden under three thousand fridge magnets, and added *cookies*. Then she went to her room to get ready for the fair.

Hairband, grubby shirt, and old jeans to withstand the cotton candy, and most important, some money. She shook a handful of coins from her piggy bank. Last year at the bake sale, someone had made the best chocolate peanut butter fudge. Hopefully it would be there again.

"When's Dad getting home?" she called out to the kitchen. "What time's supper?"

"Your dad's not home till midnight, and supper's in fifteen minutes."

Good. Turn on the computer, check for e-mail. She listened to the series of trills, chirps, and beeps as the modem dialed and checked for mail. Then came the happy sound signaling one new message, WOODEN FUSE from Auntie Jo.

What rhymed with WOODEN FUSE? Ashley was exploring a number of possibilities when the phone rang. By the time she'd finished talking to Erica, supper was ready. Before she knew it she was out the door and off to the Fall Fair.

It wasn't until the following morning that she had a chance to read her aunt's message. Then she yelled, "Mom, Dad, come and read this, quick! It says WOODEN FUSE but it means GOOD NEWS! And guess what? Auntie Jo's coming in March! She's flying to Vancouver for book signings and then she's going to Victoria and then she's coming to see us! Isn't that great?"

Dad came in and read the e-mail over Ashley's shoulder. "This is wonderful news! Gosh, how long's it been?"

"Can she stay here?"

"Of course," Mom said, joining them at the screen. "As long as we get the spare room cleaned out in time."

"I'll help," Ashley said. "I'll get started right away."

"Thirteen years, I guess." Dad answered his own question. "The last time I saw Jo was at Mom's funeral, wasn't it, Kate? That would've been 1983. And two years before that, when Dad took sick. She stayed about four months that time, helping Mom after Dad died."

Ashley grinned. "This time you'll see her without having to go to a funeral."

"Thank goodness! I was afraid the next time she came to Canada it'd be for mine. But why's she coming now? No whales to save in Revelstoke. What's the ulterior motive?"

"Stop acting so suspicious! Didn't you read the whole message? *I'm visiting Michael and his family in Victoria* — who's Michael?"

"He lived on our street when we were growing up," Dad said. "He's been Jo's best friend for years."

"OK, now this part's written for you. *It's been way too long, Ian. I'm dying to see you and Kate and meet that daughter of yours.* See? She's coming because of us!"

"Hmm. She's a kangaroo short in the upper field. Or maybe she thinks Revelstoke would be an exotic setting for one of her mysteries. She wouldn't come all this way just for us. Not Dances with Whales."

Ashley wagged a finger. "Oh, Dad. You can't fool us, can he, Mom? We know you're wild with excitement." *Wild* was pushing it. But she knew he was enormously pleased.

She was, too. She gulped down her breakfast, then rushed over to Erica's to tell her the news.

They spent the morning eating Ashley's chocolate peanut butter fudge and reliving the highlights of the Fall Fair. "I can't believe you lost your friendship ring in the cotton candy machine," Erica said. "But listen, I can make you another one, same pattern, same colors, and everything. And you know what? We should make an announcement for Monday and say that whoever found the nylon thread can keep it for flossing their teeth. But if anybody found beads in their cotton candy they should return them to me for recycling."

"I don't think so!"

"And wasn't Madame Citrona *great*? I mean, if I do say so myself. You know what I did? When Raven came I didn't let him ask a question, I just waved my hands over the crystal ball and told him he would fall in love with a black-eyed beauty. And you know what? He looked at me, straight in the eye, and he didn't even blink! Like he didn't get it! But I think my best fortune was what I told you." She lowered her voice, and with a French accent murmured, "I see in your life a great darkness . . ."

"You're such a goof!" Ashley burst out laughing.

She had no way of knowing how prophetic Erica's words would turn out to be.

21

Someone was in the room.

Ashley's heartbeat thudded in her ears. Every nerve tingled. A prickly sensation crept over her skin.

If I lie very still they won't see me. I'll be invisible if I lie very still . . . But she could feel her chest rising and falling beneath the covers. She could hear her breath. And she was still shaking from the dream that had jolted her awake.

"Mom? Dad? Is that you?" She scarcely breathed the words, yet they echoed loudly in the dark, still hush of the room.

She heard another breath. Or was it a draft of air? Had she left the window open? Had someone climbed in through the window? A cry of panic rose up in her throat.

All I have to do is reach up to the lamp, turn on the light and scream. Mom and Dad will hear — no, they won't. Dad's working nights. Mom went out and said she wouldn't be home before midnight. Was she home yet?

What time was it? If she turned her head she would be able to see her clock. If she sat up she could get the phone and call for help.

But she couldn't turn her head. She couldn't move. She could only lie on her back and stare into the darkness.

She tried to speak. "Who — what do you want?"

She saw a flicker by the window. A candle flame. Small at first, but growing steadily larger, the light pushed aside the dark and began to form a shape in the space left behind. It towered over her dresser, her desk, her chair, her bedside table, and now it was over her bed, half-blinding her with its intensity, but at the same time, confusing her with an eerie purple glow. It was now taking the shape of a person, and as she stared, spellbound, the light darkened into an enormous black shadow. An arm reached out toward her throat.

She watched it with a sort of horrified fascination, as if this was all happening at a distance, to someone else.

Slowly, slowly . . .

As the arm came closer Ashley felt a tomb-like cold, a ghostly draft stirred up by a thin, gloved hand. It touched the skin at her throat, burned her like dry ice. She whispered silently, "I'm still asleep, this is only the dream. I'll wake up like before, I'll wake up —

"AUGHHH!" She bolted to an upright position, her fist locked around the goldstone. She unclenched her fingers and turned on the lamp, almost weeping with relief as the room filled with light. Dresser, desk, chair — everything was safe and familiar, right down to the comfortable clutter on her bedside table.

Her clock showed 11:10 and as she watched, the time moved ahead to 11:11. Time hadn't stood still. Everything was normal.

The light, the shape, the hand — it was only a dream! She laughed out loud. Auntie Jo was right, a dream's just a dream. But there was something . . .

She struggled to remember the details. Was it the boy again, the boy she'd seen at Rogers Pass? Or someone else? She hadn't seen a face, only a hand. She shuddered. It had felt so cold.

She laughed again and told herself to smarten up. She hadn't really felt a hand. It was a draft, that's all. But there was something else, something she was missing . . .

Her heart pounded. Dreaming on the goldstone wasn't a game, not when it made her this terrified. She should have taken Auntie Jo's advice and stopped wearing it to sleep. But what was she afraid of? No one was forcing her. She could simply take it off.

She unfastened the chain and put the goldstone on her bedside table. Then she turned off the light and tried to go back to sleep. She tossed and turned, switched positions from back to front, from right side to left side. At some point she heard Mom come in. She thought about getting up and talking to her. By the time she'd made up her mind, Mom had gone to bed.

She curled up, she stretched out. She kicked the covers off, then pulled them back on.

Her mind raced fitfully. The boy, the hand, the snow. Raven, Erica, Auntie Jo. School, trains, mountains . . . Finally she sat up, turned the light back on, and opened the mystery lying on her bedside table. She wasn't sleepy, she might as well read as lie there thinking.

An hour later the mystery was solved. She closed the book, and as she was leaning over to turn off the lamp, she had the odd sensation of moving her arm through something more than air. Something cold . . .

She shivered and burrowed under the covers. A draft! What else? It was three o'clock in the morning, she'd been wide awake for hours, her mind was running on overtime.

Outside, a train whistle wailed. "Westbound freight," she whispered. "'Night, Dad." She followed the sound until it disappeared.

The next sound she heard was a loud knock on her door. "Get a move on, Ashley!" Mom called out. "You're running a half-hour late!"

"What?" Ashley cried. "How did that happen?" She threw back the covers and flung herself out of bed.

The events of the night flooded into her mind. A

frightening dream, someone in her room . . . She forced them out of her thoughts. There wasn't time to remember the details. But even in her haste to get ready for school, the feeling of dread remained.

22

Jonathan was confused.

The Ashley was right. The goldstone was right. There was snow on the ground so the time was right. But at the last moment, when he reached out his hand for the goldstone, something went wrong.

She screamed, Grandfather. She grabbed the goldstone and woke up screaming. I was afraid. So I shimmered away and waited. And then I went back. It was lying on her table. I reached for it again but it slipped from my grasp. I couldn't take hold.

Oh, Jonathan. You're forgetting what you are. A mist, my son. Can a mist grasp hold of a stone? Conceal it, yes. But take it away? No, no. The girl is real, Jonathan. Her gold-stone is real. You, my son, are ether real. Ethereal.

Is that why she couldn't hear me? When I saw her at the summit I tried to speak. I said her name. I said I wanted the goldstone. But then the shimmer wore off. How can I speak to her, Grandfather? How can I get hold of the goldstone?

First you must wait for the place . . .

The place! Of course, Jonathan realized. It couldn't be her room. Or the town. He had never dreamed the town.

Then you must wait for her to change her form.
You mean . . .
Yes, my son. You must wait until she shimmers.

23

"This is the stupidest assignment," Erica grumbled as she spread her books across Ashley's desk. "Write a letter to some dead ancestor, then write back pretending you're her. Or him. Stupid!"

"Do you mind if I have some room at my own desk?" Ashley pulled up an extra chair and nudged Erica out of the way. "And quit complaining. It's easy. Your own letter can say anything, just do some research on the letter your ancestor writes. What did Mrs. Irvine say? You can use old maps and photographs —"

"Uhhh . . ." Erica buried her face in her arms. "I don't have anything like that!"

"Then use an encyclopedia. Pretend your ancestor was some famous person. Like your great-great-great-grandfather was — I know! You're into fortune-telling, pretend he's the guy in that boring video we saw, what was he called? Nostril something. Remember? The guy who predicted all the catastrophes in history."

"Nostradamus!" Erica brightened. "Cool! Unless you want him."

"No, I'm not going back that far. Just don't forget it's really a history essay in disguise. So put in a lot of history stuff."

Erica groaned. "How long does it have to be? Did Mrs. Irvine say how much it counts for our final mark? What do we do to get bonus points? Can I use your computer? When's it due? Ashley, when's it due?" She poked her with a pencil.

"Ow!" Ashley scowled. "Just do it, Erica."

"When's it due?"

Ashley consulted her notebook. "December the thirteenth."

"That's two weeks away!" Erica exclaimed. "Why're we doing it now?"

"Because! Gosh, you're annoying."

"Did you tell Raven I liked him yet? What did he say?" She gave Ashley another poke. "Hmm? I asked you ages ago, Ash! You went skiing with him and everything, you had a million chances! So what did he say? Does he like me? And how come he's got such an attitude all of a sudden? He got three detentions last week for mouthing off."

"Erica, be quiet!"

There were a few moments of silence. Then Erica flung down her pencil and said, "This is hopeless. Can I play that new computer game you got?"

"Yeah . . . No, wait! Go on the Internet and find out how to make ink."

"What?"

"You know, ink. I'm going to use a feather for a quill pen and make my own ink. For when my ancestor writes back, see? That'll get me bonus points. So will you?"

"Only if we can have some more ice cream. And only if you let me play the game after. OK? Deal?"

"Aughh!" Ashley raised her head and screamed. "Why do I even like you, Erica? You're driving me crazy!"

"Ice cream?" Erica grinned.

"All right, all right. What kind do you want, rocky road or royal purple cherry?"

"Rocky purple cherry!" she called as Ashley left the room.

A short time later they'd both finished their ice cream — two scoops of each flavor — and were settled into their tasks. While Erica clicked at the computer keyboard, Ashley wrote her letter.

Dear Karin,
You don't know me, and I don't know much about you. Only that you're a distant relative, my great-aunt to be concise. And we've got something in common. Auntie Jo gave me the goldstone that once belonged to you. It was the best birthday present I ever got. I would like to know if you

dreamed on it and if you saw the future. So I hope you write back —

She stopped, pen poised over the paper. Erica was right, this was a stupid assignment. Writing to a dead person and expecting an answer? She crossed out the last two sentences, then carried on.

Auntie Jo never met you, but pretty soon I get to meet her. I feel like I know her already. It's weird how you can get to know somebody without ever meeting them in person.

"Hey, Ash," Erica said just then. "You're not going to like this. You have to mash walnut hulls and boil them, and then add salt and vinegar."

"What are you talking about?"

"Making ink! Did you forget already? But there's an easier way, wanna hear it? You use lemon juice."

"That's for invisible ink."

"Well, yeah! Get your ancestor to write some highly secret stuff and make Mrs. Irvine figure it out. You can include directions. All she has to do is hold the letter over a flame. She'll love it, and you'll get double bonus points!"

Not bad, Ashley thought. Turn the whole assignment into a game. But throw in lots of historical facts so she'd get a really good mark. And that was easy. All she had to do was find out from Mom what Revelstoke was like a hundred years ago. She gave herself a mental pat on the back for choosing an ancestor that had once lived in the very same town.

Auntie Jo might know some more, not about Revelstoke, but about Karin. Maybe she'd seen pictures or something when she was a kid.

"I gotta go, Ash." Erica interrupted her thoughts. "Phone me tonight, OK? And tell me what Raven said."

"He said you were a pain."

"Ha! I always know when you're kidding. You try to keep a straight face, but your eyes crinkle up at the corners."

"Good-bye, Erica."

"Wait a sec, I almost forgot my homework. And by the way, don't forget my birthday next Saturday. And my sleepover. It starts at five o'clock and I'll remind you every single day. And tell Raven I think he's cute!"

"GOOD-BYE!"

Once Erica was gone, Ashley went into the kitchen and set the table for supper. She grilled her mother about Revelstoke in the olden days and was promised a whole stack of photocopied material from the museum. The bonus points were adding up.

After supper she went to the computer and e-mailed Auntie Jo, asking for any information about Karin. She sent the message with the subject, KELP CHEESE, then watched the winged toasters flying across her screen. It was about time for a new screen-saver. The fish one was neat, or maybe the gems and precious stones?

She absentmindedly reached up to touch her pendant and gave an exclamation of surprise. The goldstone was gone.

24

Where was it?

Ashley desperately tried to think what might have happened. Had she worn the goldstone to school that day? She retraced her steps, beginning with the previous night when the dream had awakened her. What had she done? She'd removed the pendant, placed it on her bedside table, tried to go back to sleep, then somehow overslept. After that there'd been such a rush to get to school she hadn't had time to put on the pendant.

So where was it? Not on the bedside table. She removed everything — mystery book, phone, clock, box of tissues, various pairs of earrings, gum wrappers, a half-empty bag of chips, and the stained glass picture of a hummingbird she still hadn't hung in her window.

Had she unconsciously picked it up and set it down somewhere? She searched her dresser and jewelry box, her desk, the wastepaper basket and window sill. She looked along the baseboards and in the closet. Nothing.

Had it rolled under the bed? She lifted the ruffled bed skirt and crawled underneath. A duffle bag, a couple of mismatched socks, more gum wrappers, one shrunken apple, a field of dust bunnies. But no goldstone.

She crawled back out and sneezed. Then sat on her bed and tried to think where it might have gone. "Nowhere!" she cried. "It should be right where I left it!"

Unless . . .

A horrible suspicion began to form in her mind.

Erica. Was it possible . . .

No! No way would Erica take the goldstone.

But who else had been in Ashley's room? Who had both motive and opportunity? Erica had asked a thousand times if she could borrow the pendant. She could've slipped it into her pocket when Ashley went to get the ice cream. There was such a mess on the bedside table she probably figured Ashley wouldn't even notice it was gone.

A surge of anger replaced the tight knot in her chest. Erica, her best friend — how *could* she! Furious, she grabbed the phone and dialed Erica's number.

"We're sorry we can't come to the phone right now —"

Ashley hung up on the machine. Erica wasn't out. She was probably asleep. She'd probably gone to bed at six o'clock to make good and sure she had a full night's worth of dreams. Ashley hoped they'd be nightmares.

"Get your ink made?" Erica asked the next morning.

"Not yet," Ashley replied and pushed her mouth into a smile. She was determined to act normal. If Erica didn't give back the goldstone or say anything about it, then Ashley would bring up the subject. Meanwhile, she'd wait and see what happened.

By the time school was out Erica still hadn't given it back. She hadn't even mentioned it.

"You wanna go skating tonight, Ash?" she asked as they were packing up their things. "Since it's parent interviews tomorrow and there's no school. So I know I'm allowed. Everybody's going, Clipper and Scout and Steph. And Raven." She clasped a hand over her heart and gave an exaggerated sigh. "So you wanna come? We're meeting at the arena at 7:00."

"I'll think about it," Ashley said.

They walked home together as usual, Erica chattering away about how much she liked Raven and how smart he was. Unlike Scout and his boring collection of Boy Scout badges, and that gross Clipper who only knew how to belch. Then she fast-forwarded to her birthday on Saturday and how she couldn't wait for her sleepover . . . If she thought Ashley was being unusually quiet, she didn't mention it. And by the time they reached her street, she still hadn't breathed a word about the goldstone.

Ashley was steeling herself to bring up the subject when Erica said, "You wanna come over for leftover pizza? It's Hawaiian, with ham and pineapple. And it's really, really good."

Ashley couldn't resist. Now it'll come, she thought. Peace offering of pizza, then confession, then apology. I won't get angry or upset. I'll just say thank you, and that'll be the end of that.

When they got to Erica's, Erica took the pizza out of the fridge, grabbed a couple of cold sodas, and led Ashley into her room. She promptly kicked off her shoes and sprawled across her bed, math books propped against her pillow. "You can have my desk," she said.

"Where is it?" Ashley asked.

"The desk?" Erica swallowed a mouthful of pizza and laughed. "Where it always is, *duhh*."

Ashley's mouth tightened. "You know what I mean. The goldstone, Erica. Where is it?" She hadn't meant to blurt it out like that. She'd planned to wait a bit longer and give Erica a chance to explain. Talk about good intentions.

"So that's why you aren't wearing it today," Erica said. "You haven't lost it, have you?"

"No, I haven't lost it. Somebody took it. And I'd really, really like it back."

"What?" Erica's jaw dropped, and her eyes widened with disbelief. "Are you —? No. You're not, seriously, accusing me."

Ashley ignored the hurt look on Erica's face. "You were the only person in my room yesterday, and I know how much you wanted to borrow it. So . . ." She faltered, wishing she'd kept quiet, but knowing it was too late to take back her words.

"I don't believe this! You're actually accusing me of stealing?"

"What am I supposed to think? You're the only person who had the chance!"

Erica bolted from her bed. "Why don't you search my room? Go on, do a search. I'll make it easy for you. I'll even help." She threw her half-eaten pizza onto the plate, crossed to her dresser, and began opening the drawers. One by one she emptied them, hurling their contents to the floor.

Her voice rose to a shout. "See? Nothing there. Go on, Ashley, look through my jewelry box, and my desk drawers, don't forget those. And under my pillow, and what about under my mattress? Go on, look!"

"All right, I will." Ashley searched under the mattress and under the bed and in the closet. She ran her hand across the top of the bookshelf. She shook out every one of Erica's shoes in case she'd hidden the pendant inside the toe. It was only when Erica started screaming at her to search the whole house because, of course, she must have hidden it in her sister's bedroom or in her father's workroom or why not inside her mother's sewing machine — it was only then that

Ashley stopped. She looked at the mess in Erica's room and gasped. "What am I doing?"

"You should say, What've I *done*? Are you satisfied? Now get out."

"What's going on in there?" Erica's mother had just come home and was calling out from the kitchen. "Girls, what's the problem?"

"Nothing!" They both answered at once. Then Erica scooped up Ashley's untouched pizza slices and slammed them into her chest. "Get out."

Ashley grabbed her coat and left without a word. Her favorite sweater was probably ruined with ham and cheese and tomato sauce, but that was the least of her worries. She kept telling herself it wasn't her fault. She'd had the goldstone and now it was gone. And Erica was responsible.

She spent the evening fuming. All her friends would be at the arena, skating and having a fabulous time. Steph would be bragging about her figure-skating lessons and showing off her triple sow cows or whatever. Scout would be telling everybody for the millionth time how he'd earned a badge for ice fishing. Erica would be acting like a goof, trying to get Raven's attention. Maybe she'd do her fainting thing and crack her head on the ice. Ashley almost smiled until she realized that Erica would be having so much fun. And *she* was the one who should be stuck at home and miserable. Not Ashley.

To make matters worse, Raven came over the next morning and told her she shouldn't have accused Erica without any proof.

"I don't need proof!" Ashley retorted. "There's no other explanation."

"There's got to be. Things don't just vanish. You want me to come in and have a look?"

"No! And thanks a lot for taking Erica's side!"

"You might as well know, everybody's on her side."

"So that's what you guys did last night? You all listened to Erica and decided it was *my* fault?"

"Look, you don't just accuse somebody. Especially not your best friend."

"Well, she's not my best friend anymore. And you can tell her that, for all I care! Now that you two are so, so —"

"So *what*?"

"And another thing. You know why your dad moved away? Because of *you*! And you know why my dad takes you places? Not because he likes you. It's only because he feels sorry for you!" She slammed the door in his face and went inside.

Talk about a lousy, rotten, horrible day. The only thing that could possibly save it would be a message from Auntie Jo. But there was no new mail.

She opened the website Erica had bookmarked a few weeks earlier. Supernatural stuff, fortune-telling, dream analysis. Maybe she'd learn how to put a curse on a former best friend.

All that we see or seem is but a dream within a dream . . . The quote from Edgar Allan Poe was followed by a dream dictionary. Ashley felt a flicker of hope. Maybe this could shed some light on the goldstone dreams. *Snow.* First she'd look up snow. She followed the instructions, clicked S, and discovered that a dream about snow suggested that she, or someone else in her dream, was emotionally cold and unresponsive. "That's helpful," she snarled. Her spirits dropped.

More surfing revealed Tarot on line, directions on how to tell fortunes with poker, and how to get spells and curses from Clarissa, a clairvoyant cat. "Right," she muttered. "And I'm an alien."

Another site allowed her to ask a question about her future to a member of the Oracles Society. She chose one, typed in her name, her birthday and the question, *Will I find my missing goldstone?* Then she pressed *Submit*. Seconds later she received the answer.

Your oracle says:

NO!

It went on to tell her to get a life.

She left the site in disgust and checked her e-mail again. *You have no new mail.* She could almost hear the server laughing.

What future would she dream tonight if she had her goldstone? What was Erica dreaming? If she concentrated really hard, maybe her thoughts would be transmitted to the goldstone and from there, straight into Erica's brain. Tomorrow she'd write a new question to the Oracles Society. *How can I get rid of Erica?*

She felt her face crumple. No, she wouldn't. She'd forgive Erica in a minute. Losing the goldstone was bad enough. Losing her best friend was worse.

As for Raven . . . All day long she tried to forget what she'd said. And the look on his face, as if she'd kicked him hard in the stomach. He'll know it's not true, she kept telling herself. He'll know I didn't mean it.

But what if he believed that a part of it was true? He would never forgive her.

The next morning Ashley left later than usual to avoid meeting Erica on the way to school. At recess and lunch she looked on as Erica and Raven kidded around with their other friends. How was it that Erica was in the wrong yet *she* was the one left out?

She hoped the goldstone was giving Erica a horrible future, but it seemed to be doing just the opposite as far as her interest in Raven was concerned. Ashley watched the two of them together and felt an unexpected twinge of jealousy. Erica was right. Raven was good-looking and smart and funny. She'd never noticed before. Now it was too late. He avoided her like the plague, and if she did catch his eye, he immediately looked away.

She kept thinking, It'll pass. Raven'll come over to see Dad and he'll realize what I said wasn't true. Erica will give back the goldstone and make up some lame excuse like it accidentally fell into her pocket. And things will get back to normal.

On Friday, when Steph handed her a note, Ashley unfolded it eagerly, certain that Erica was going to admit everything and say she was sorry. Instead, she'd written, *My birthday sleepover tomorrow is canceled. For everybody whose initials are A.G.*

Ashley scrawled *GOOD* at the bottom of the note and sent it back.

She tried to swallow her disappointment, but it stuck in her throat like a chunk of hard-boiled egg. They'd been planning Erica's birthday for weeks, what they'd order at the restaurant when they went out to dinner, what videos they'd rent, how they were going to stay awake talking all night. But what did she expect? Of course Erica wouldn't want her to come.

The day dragged on, bringing the week to an end. The worst week of her entire life.

"You seem a bit blue," Mom said at dinner that night. "Something happen at school?"

Ashley stabbed at a fish stick. "Erica's sick. The sleepover's canceled."

"Oh, I'm sorry. You were so looking forward to it."

"Not really," Ashley mumbled.

"You're not coming down with something, are you? You haven't touched your supper."

"I'm not hungry." She pushed back her chair and took her plate to the sink.

"Your turn to clean up," Mom said.

"It's always my turn!" Ashley flared up angrily. "And I'm doing it, all right?"

"Fine. And thank you." Mom put her plate on the counter. "Wrap up the rest of that pie, will you? Dad can have it when he comes home. He's on the late shift again."

"Like that's something new."

"What's that?"

"Nothing! And I suppose he's spending Sunday with Raven. How come I never get to do anything?" She turned the water tap full blast, rinsed the dishes, and loaded them savagely into the dishwasher. "Is that why you called me Ashley? 'Cause you wanted a boy? That's what it is, you know, a stupid boy's name. I saw it in a book."

Mom came up behind her. "What's that about a book? Sorry, I was in the other room."

"Nothing! For the millionth time." She took the dishrag and attacked the table and countertops, seething inside. What am I doing? If it wasn't for that little thief . . .

The cleanup finished, she stomped into her room and switched on the computer. *You have no new mail.* Even her aunt had deserted her.

Dejected, she went into the bathroom, filled up the tub, and poured in the rest of her mother's raspberry frost bath foam. She soaked for twenty minutes, hoping to come up with a plan regarding Erica and a way to take back what she'd said to Raven. All she got was wrinkly skin.

She dragged herself into the living room, turned on the TV, and channel surfed for an hour, flipping from travel tips to the music channel to an old Tarzan movie to a program on how to stuff mushrooms.

"Ashley, for goodness sake turn it down or make up your mind!" Mom shouted from the den. "I can't concentrate on anything!"

Ashley turned off the TV. The library was still open, she might as well walk over and check out some more mysteries. Might as well have something to read since she didn't have any friends.

On the way home she deliberately walked past Erica's house. Erica would look out the window and see her, then come running outside and say, Here's your goldstone, Ashley. I don't blame you for being mad, I never meant to take it. You're still my best, best, best, best friend . . .

Naturally that didn't happen.

Motive and opportunity. Erica, the prime suspect. No, make that crime suspect.

As soon as she got home she slumped down on her bed and tried to decide which new book to read first. Decision made, she was propping up her pillows to get more comfortable when she happened to glance at her bedside table. What she saw made her gasp with astonishment. The goldstone was back.

"Thank you, thank you!" She clasped the pendant and ran into the den. "Mom, when was Erica here?"

"Erica wasn't here. You said she was sick."

"No, she's not. I just made that up because — Ohhh! Never mind. I know she was here 'cause she brought back the goldstone."

"No, honey, I put the goldstone on your table."

"*What?*" Ashley's stomach lurched. "You — you took my goldstone?"

"Of course not! I was washing the bedskirts and duvet covers this morning, and when I was taking yours off the bed the goldstone rolled out. It must have got trapped in a pleat or something, underneath the covers. How long was it missing?"

"The whole week!"

"You never said it was gone. Oh, dear. When you asked about Erica, you didn't think . . ."

"I've just had the worst time! I blamed Erica, then everybody started to hate me. But I don't know how I missed it! I searched that room like you wouldn't believe!"

There was only one thing to do. She went back to her room and picked up the phone. Then she took several deep breaths and dialed Erica's number.

Her voice froze when Erica answered. She cleared her throat, took another breath, then said quickly, "Don't hang up, it's me. Ashley."

There was a long pause. "So?"

"So I'm phoning to tell you I've got it back. The goldstone, I mean. Mom found it. It was — it was in my room the whole time."

"So?"

"So I'm — I'm sorry," Ashley stammered. "I should've known."

"Yup. You should've." With that, Erica hung up.

Ashley lowered the phone. She blinked and a tear rolled down her cheek.

Maybe if she talked to Raven. She would explain about finding the goldstone and apologize for the hateful things she'd said. She was halfway through dialing when she remembered he'd gone to Golden for the weekend. She would have to wait till Monday, then go to school and face everyone at the same time.

25

Ashley walked to the park, enjoying the crunch of fresh snow beneath her feet. There had been a heavy snowfall the night before, but the morning had dawned sunny and clear. She almost felt happy.

The previous two weeks had been a nightmare. She had worn the goldstone to school, hoping that things would return to normal once it was known she'd made a mistake. She'd admitted it and said she was sorry, but things weren't the same. Erica and the others weren't as cold as they had been, but they were nowhere close to being warm. And when she'd taken Raven aside and apologized for what she'd said, he'd merely shrugged and walked away.

She lost interest in her history project and barely

received a passing grade. She quit the school choir three days before the Christmas concert and stayed home the day of the grade seven skating party. What was the point? No one would skate with her.

She made one final attempt on the last day of school and invited Erica over the following night for videos. Sorry, Erica had told her. I'm going to Steph's party. Weren't you invited? The memory of her laughter still rankled.

In spite of her glum mood, Ashley couldn't help but notice the festive atmosphere in the neighborhood. Houses were strung with lights, wreaths decorated the doors, Christmas trees glittered in the windows. Kids were outside building snowmen and making snow angels, while parents shoveled walks and stairs.

The hill near the park was a festival in itself, a colorful tangle of people and dogs and sliding objects, from sleds and toboggans to oversized Frisbees and garbage can lids. She spotted a group of her classmates, laughing and throwing snowballs. A loud shriek told her that Erica was among them.

So was Clipper. "Hey, there's Ashley!" he yelled. "Guess you knew all this snow was coming, hey, Ash? What's next? Is it going to melt?" He gave his crow-like laugh and the others joined in.

Ashley felt her face grow hot. What was the use? They'd never let her forget, never. She turned and started to head for home.

Suddenly she felt something hit the back of her head. Ignore it, she told herself. It's only a snowball, a snowball won't kill you. She straightened her shoulders and carried on as another snowball pelted her in the back. And another. She started to run.

"Hey, wait up! You ruby-coated snicker!"

Ashley turned and saw Erica running toward her with a snowball in each hand. Without stopping to think, Ashley scooped up a handful of snow and charged at Erica, her breath coming in loud, painful gasps. "Can't a person make a mistake?" she shouted. "I said I was sorry!" She grabbed Erica's coat and pushed her down, then washed her face with snow.

"Stop it!" Erica screamed. She lunged up, grabbed Ashley by the shoulders, flipping and straddling her in the snow.

Ashley dug in with her fingers, pressed a handful of snow into a ball, and threw the snowball at Erica's face.

"Oww!" Erica loosened her grip, but she wasn't giving up easily. The two rolled over and over in the snow, arms locked around each other.

"Get offa me!" Ashley yelled. "I'm warning you, you —"

"You, what? Heh, ugly face? You lousy —"

"You're a lousy joke!" Ashley hurled back. "A blue-livered, cow-eyed joke. And you make a rotten fortune-teller, Madame Citrona. Aughh!"

Erica released her hold and started to shake. "Stop it! Just stop it!" Her shaking turned into giggles.

"What's so funny?"

"You're going to make me wet my pants!" Erica stumbled to her feet, doubled over with laughter.

Ashley sat up in the snow, then she, too, began to

laugh. "Well, you're —" She stopped abruptly and stared at Erica's face. It had turned ghostly pale, as if all the life had been sucked out of it. "Are you OK? You look as if . . . as if you're going to pass out."

"Nice try!" Erica laughed. "Why, you think you threw a snowball hard enough to make me unconcious? That'll be the day. You throw like a two year old. I didn't even feel it."

"But I saw —" The image of a lifeless face flashed into her mind. But even as she spoke, Ashley could see that Erica's face was its usual animated color. "Never mind."

"You dreaming again? Oops, better not bring that up." Erica looked away and fumbled with the zipper on her coat. Then she turned back to Ashley and extended a hand. "Truce?"

"Truce." Ashley clasped Erica's hand and let herself be pulled up.

For several moments they concentrated on brushing the snow off their clothing. Ashley wasn't sure what the next step or the next words should be. How many times did she need to say she was sorry? They both broke the silence at once.

"Do you want to —"

"Are you going —"

They looked at each other and laughed. "You first," Erica said.

"Are you going carolling tomorrow night?"

Erica nodded happily. "Do you want to come over to my house right now? You can help me wrap presents."

"Sure!" Ashley grinned. All the same, she felt a bit

apprehensive as they walked to Erica's, as if they had only just met and weren't certain how they would get along. It might not be so easy, to slip back to the way things used to be. The ice was broken, but it could freeze up again at any time.

"Ashley, aren't you listening? You never change!"

"Sorry. What did you say?"

"I just said, I dream about Raven every single night. Oops, I forgot. I won't mention dreams ever again. Except to ask one little question. Have you had any good future dreams lately?"

"No . . ." How could she explain it? Since the night she'd felt the presence of someone in her room she'd been afraid to fall asleep, let alone dream on the goldstone. She double-checked the lock on her window. She found the night light she'd had as a baby and kept it on. She left her door slightly ajar.

"Well, Ash? Have you? You can tell your best, best friend."

"I don't wear the goldstone at night anymore," she said, and left it at that.

Still, she couldn't dismiss the feeling that in one of her dreams, she had seen a deathly white face. It was another sliver, dreamed and forgotten, then wham! There it was, clear in her mind. But whose face was it in the dream? Was it Erica's? Or was it her own?

26

The time passed quickly in the weeks leading up to Auntie Jo's visit.

In January, Ashley took a ski-touring course to break in the alpine touring gear she'd received for Christmas. Dad was as excited as she was. "You'll need the wider skis for the backcountry," he said. "Your cross-country skis are too light, especially in Rogers Pass. And see how these bindings work? They let your heel lift up when you're climbing, but they lock down when you're going downhill. Perfect! And the high-top boots — you're all set, kid! We won't be able to keep up with you!"

"You mean, you and Raven?" Raven had got touring skis the year before and had already spent many weekends with Dad in the backcountry. "Can I start coming with you?" Ashley asked. "And don't say it's a guy thing."

Dad chucked her under the chin and laughed. "Don't tell me you're jealous. Or could it be that you want to spend more time with Raven? And all this time I thought it was me."

"Da-ad! Honestly." To tell the truth, she wasn't sure. At least Raven was talking to her again.

He'd been horrible at school. The previous week, for example; the substitute teacher was doing a science lesson on the inner ear and had just reached the cochlea when Raven blurted out, "Did you know that turkey vultures poop on their feet to cool off?"

The teacher gave him a stunned look, obviously trying to figure out the connection between turkey vultures and the cochlea. Before she could say anything, Clipper started in on one of his belching marathons, and Erica fainted. The afternoon went downhill from there.

The substitute gave the whole class a detention, even though Raven had started the ruckus, and guaranteed that when Mrs. Irvine came back there'd be "hell to pay." There was. The class got another detention. Their noon-hour dance was canceled. Raven, since he already had three strikes against him for unacceptable behavior, received a two-day suspension.

And at home? Practically every other weekend he got himself grounded. And was it a coincidence that those weekends were the ones when he was supposed to go to Golden? Somehow Ashley didn't think so. But he was always around when her dad was free.

"I can't stand it!" Erica said one day. "He's over at your house all the time!"

"Yeah, for one second. Long enough to get in the car and go skiing with Dad."

"And you! You lucky bum."

"I don't go all the time."

"I still think you and Raven were switched when you were babies. Hey, here's a thought! What if your aunt, that you like so much, is really your mother? And what if your father —"

"Stop watching so many soap operas!" Ashley laughed and gave Erica a swat on the head. "Let me keep my family the way it is."

One morning in late February, Ashley woke to the song of the varied thrush. The sound was unmistakable — a long, haunting, whistled note, followed by a pause, then another note, lower in pitch. Its meaning, too, was unmistakable. Even though there was still a ton of snow, the arrival of the varied thrush was the first sign of spring. March was around the corner, and Auntie Jo would soon be there.

In anticipation of her aunt's visit, Ashley decided to try another dream on the goldstone. "No bad dreams," she whispered before falling asleep. "Nothing scary like the last time. Just a glimpse of my brilliant future. And a glimpse of Auntie Jo. So I won't be too surprised."

She fell asleep and dreamed. When she woke the next morning all she could remember was a deep and muffled darkness.

On the last Saturday of February, Mom hijacked

Ashley on her way to Erica's and said, "Remember that promise you made? About cleaning out the spare room?"

"Mo-om!" Ashley groaned. "We need a backhoe to clean out that room."

"You offered, honey."

"I know, I know. I'll do it right away."

"Seems to me you said that three months ago. But now that we're getting close to the time . . ."

"Yes!" Ashley exclaimed. "It's only three weeks now, isn't it? Guess we better get started." She phoned Erica to say she'd be over a little later and headed off to the spare room.

The room was such a disaster she wished she'd never offered to help. "What is all this stuff?" she asked as they began carting out boxes. "And why are we taking it to the basement? Now the basement's going to be an even bigger mess."

"We'll worry about that later. For now, as the song goes, 'Tote that barge and lift that bale.'"

"'Ol' Man River' to you, too, Mom. Euf! This weighs a ton."

"Speak to your father. Twenty years of railway magazines and he can't part with a single one."

"Oh, right. Blame him. Seems to me I just lugged a million hysterical weeklies downstairs."

"I think you mean historical."

"Whatever!" Ashley heaved a sigh and hoisted another heavy box.

By noon they could see the sofa bed and the carpet. "You can run along," Mom said. "I'll do the vacuuming and dusting later."

"What's in there?" Ashley pointed to a trunk, previously hidden behind a stack of rolled-up carpets and books of wallpaper samples.

"Ohhh!" Mom smiled. "That old trunk! I'd completely forgotten. Your dad and I had a quick look when we were sorting out your grandma's house, after she died. I'd always meant to get back to it, but somehow . . . I don't know, it was upsetting at first, then something always got in the way. Well, I know Jo'll be interested. There's family albums, books, all sorts of treasures, I bet."

"I'll take a look," Ashley said. "Maybe tomorrow."

She got sidetracked the next day and went skiing instead. The trunk was put on hold the following week, too, what with homework and Steph's sleepover and play rehearsals for the school's spring production. And by the third week of March the trunk was totally forgotten in the excitement of her aunt's arrival.

27

All day long Ashley wondered what her aunt would be like. She knew her from letters and e-mails and the occasional phone conversation, but in person? Maybe she'd be different in real life, shy and hard to talk to. Maybe she'd be the opposite, snobby and arrogant.

"Stop worrying!" Erica said as they were walking home from school. "So what if she's famous? She's not going to have three heads, is she? And she's not a kid, she's a grown-up. You're not going to be hanging out with her. You don't even have to share your bedroom, like I have to do when my bratty cousins come for holidays. Look, the worst thing that can happen is you'll hate her. But so what? She'll be gone in a month."

"I know. That's what I'm afraid of. That I won't like her. And she'll go away and I won't want to write to her anymore. And what if she doesn't like me?"

"Know what, Ashley? You think too much. 'What if, what if' — who cares 'what if?'"

When they reached the corner where Erica turned off, Ashley grabbed Erica's arm and said, "Don't go! Come home with me and meet her!"

"Later, Ash. I can't handle celebrities on an empty stomach. And she might be, you know, *really* weird. Pierced tongue, shaved head, daggers tattooed on her face — relax! I'm kidding!" She gave Ashley a pat on the shoulder and, with a parting "Good luck," continued on her way.

Ashley needn't have worried. As far as appearance was concerned, her aunt looked much like the photo on her book jackets. Except for the six multicolored studs climbing up one ear and the hair color.

"What do you call it?" Dad was saying as Ashley came in. "Flaming tangerine? Locomotive red?"

"You don't call it gray," Jo retorted, tugging on her brother's beard. "Oh, yes, I can see those bits of gray showing through."

Before he could respond, he spotted Ashley standing in the doorway. "Here she is! Come and meet your famous aunt. Have you ever seen such hair? We'll have to switch her name from Dances with Whales to Dances with Parrots."

"Ashley!" Jo gave her a warm smile. "It's wonderful to meet you in person. As for this old guy —" she gestured to her brother. "Dances with Whales? Is he always like that?"

Ashley laughed. "He's usually worse."

"Then we've got a lot of work to do."

"Poor guy," Mom said. "Three against one. Ian, are you sure you don't want to cancel your holidays and go back to work?"

"Nope, I thrive on being picked on. But listen. We've got another couple of hours before dinner, Jo. What's your pleasure? You want to relax, have a tour of the town, go for a quick ski or toboggan run, or visit our famous railway museum or our equally fascinating historical museum? Whatever you like."

"Careful, Auntie Jo," Ashley warned. "He's got everything planned for the next month, right down to the last minute."

Jo smiled fondly at her brother. "Sounds great, Ian. Look, before I forget . . ." She rummaged in her bag and handed Ashley a brown feather, white on the tip, with a pattern of black bands flowing along the shaft. "It's a kookaburra's tail feather," she explained. "They splash around in my birdbath and have a terrific time. And the sound they make! You can't help but laugh, even though they wake you up at the crack of dawn."

"Do they really sound like they're laughing? We learned a song in school that goes, 'Laugh, kookaburra, laugh, kookaburra,' something like that. So do they?"

"Sure do. First one starts, kind of low, but getting higher and higher. Like this. *Kookoo kookoo kaakaa kaakaa* . . . then another joins in and before you know it the whole bush is filled with laughter, like a bunch of chimps going berserk. Try it."

Everyone joined in until Mom clasped her hands to her ears and yelled, "Stop! We get the idea!"

"Now we can add bird impersonations to the list of things to do," Dad said. "So what's it to be, Jo? You want to relax —"

"Da-ad! You don't need to repeat everything!"

"Actually . . ." Jo thought for a moment. "What I really feel like is a walk along the river. How about it, Ashley? You want to come and fill me in on your dad's latest eccentricities?"

"That could take awhile. How long before supper, Mom? Don't start without us."

"Here, Jo. Take these." Dad handed her his binoculars. "You never know what you might see."

Jo looked skeptical. "This part of the world, I don't know . . . It reminds me of something Oscar Wilde once said. 'I only know two kinds of birds. One is the sparrow and one isn't.' But thanks. Just give me a second to put on my winter gear."

Twenty minutes later she appeared in snowmobile pants, parka, tuque, mittens, and fur-lined boots. "Don't you dare laugh," she said. "I'm not used to the cold."

Ashley and her parents exchanged amused glances. The temperature was mild to them, about one degree above freezing. If Jo thought that was cold, it was a good thing she hadn't come in January.

Once outside, Ashley set a brisk pace down the street, then led her aunt to the dyke along the river.

"Brrr!" Jo stamped her feet and rubbed her hands together. "I'd forgotten the meaning of cold. But it's kind of nice, you know — a bracing wind, the crunch of snow, the river, the mountains . . . It smells so fresh and clean. No wonder you love it here. And it's a great change for me. When I left Perth a couple of weeks ago it was so hot! Nothing like January, though. My poor tomatoes literally boiled on the vine and my candles melted into puddles of wax. Fair dinkum!"

"Fair what?"

"Fair dinkum! It's an Aussie expression for 'no kidding.'" She laughed. "Don't worry, I wasn't saying anything rude."

"Do you want to walk along the dyke a ways?" Ashley asked.

"Sure! That'll warm me up. And I see you've brought your binoculars. Holler if you spot an interesting bird, all right? I want to impress Ian with some bird trivia."

"Don't mention the word trivia! My friend Raven bores everybody with his useless facts. Like right now, if he was here he'd tell you all about the Columbia River, how long it is and how deep and how many gallons of water and what kinds of fish and on and on and on. He drives us crazy."

A train whistle sounded, and Ashley pointed to the freight train crossing the bridge at the far end of town. "Hopper car, hopper car, piggy-back, robot, robot, piggy-back . . . Mostly hoppers. They're grain cars, the ones with the curved sides. The piggy-backs, they're the ones that carry the truck trailers, and the robots, that's what you call the locomotives in the middle of the train. That's my trivia for the day. I'm a train watcher."

"Do much whale watching?" Jo asked.

The question took Ashley by surprise. "Not here!"

"Well, no," Jo laughed. "I guess I meant when you've gone to Vancouver Island."

Ashley shook her head.

"That's what you call a *non sequitur*. You're talking about trains and I bring up whales. Makes sense, right? I actually thought of the whales because of the goldstone, which makes even more sense. But it will." She smiled. "I'm pleased you're wearing it, by the way."

Ashley smiled back. Thank goodness it wasn't still missing.

"You've been dreaming on it, too," Jo continued. "Thanks for telling me about them. Your dreams, I mean." She paused, wondering how much she should say. She'd been with Ashley less than an hour and so far things seemed to be going well. The last thing she wanted was for Ashley to think she was overreacting.

"I dreamed of whales before I ever saw them," she said. "There was a whale stranded on the beach. Then another and another until the sand was covered with whales. I saw the wide mouth of a river and birds that looked like pelicans. For a minute the dream was clear, but then it faded into a blur of whales and sand and sea and sky. And I felt this, I don't know how to describe it, this feeling of quiet, in spite of the whales thrashing about. A feeling that I belonged there. And I woke up thinking, That's it, that's where I've got to go. Except I didn't have a clue where it was. So I forgot the dream and the beach and the whales. Until I ended up in Western Australia, in a little town called Augusta. And there it was. The beach and the sand and the whales. Hard to believe that was just over ten years ago."

"Were the whales really stranded on the beach?" Ashley wondered.

"Yes," Jo replied. "One hundred and fourteen whales, all stranded, all alive. And we rescued them. The whole town came out to help. Everyone adopted a whale. I stayed with mine all day and all night, keeping it moist, keeping the blow hole clear. It was July, our winter, and pretty cold. Eventually we got all the whales back out to sea. It took three full days. The first attempt failed. Oh, it was heartbreaking, how the whales all swam back and got themselves stranded again. But the second attempt was a success. I swam out with them, along with some other board riders. Imagine, shepherding a pod of whales! It was really something. And ninety-six were saved."

"Why do they do that, strand themselves?"

"No one knows for sure. They're very social, these particular whales. If one of the pod's in trouble, the others come to help."

By now they were on the part of the dyke that ran by the Greenbelt, where the Illecillewaet River joined the Columbia. "Oh, look!" Ashley exclaimed, raising her binoculars. "It's a — wait a sec." She looked through the binoculars, opening and closing the tubes until the two viewfields fused together into one circle. Then she adjusted the focus. "It's a trumpeter swan! You don't usually see them on moving water, mostly in the wetlands by the airport. Dad'll be here in a minute when we tell him. See it? And there's something else . . ."

On the far shore she could see the glow of a faint purple light. And coming into focus, an outstretched hand. She gasped and quickly lowered the binoculars.

"What is it?" Jo asked.

Ashley's mouth had gone dry. Fear curdled in her stomach. She wanted to throw up. But she looked at her aunt and suddenly felt foolish. What was she going to do, tell Auntie Jo she was seeing things? That would make a good impression.

She swallowed her fear and gave a lame laugh. "I thought I saw another swan. I guess it was nothing."

A circle of purple light, an outstretched hand . . . She'd seen that hand before. Reaching toward her throat, in the darkness of her room, in the middle of the night.

28

Jonathan was impatient.

He knew he had to wait. The right time, the right place . . .

Still, he was impatient.

He shimmered down from the mountains and into the town. Not to take back the goldstone, not yet, but simply to watch and to wait.

He saw the Ashley on the street, by the school, near the railway station. Sometimes with others, sometimes alone.

One day, late in the afternoon, he saw her by the river. The urge to touch the goldstone was too powerful to resist. Jonathan reached out a hand, imagining the feel of the smooth, glassy stone, set aglow by the

warmth of her skin. He took a step forward —
Wait, my son. Wait until she shimmers . . .

Jonathan stopped. Grandfather was right.
He had to wait until she shimmered.

29

"I can't stop shivering," Auntie Jo said. "Does that restaurant over there have hot chocolate? It's time to get out of the cold."

Soon they were breathing in the tangy scent of malt vinegar, eating French fries, and drinking hot chocolate. Ashley finished the last of her fries, then drew a snowflake on the steamed-up window. "I loved making paper snowflakes when I was little," she said.

"Me, too," Jo smiled. "That was a long time ago."

"It's weird, that time difference between Australia and here," Ashley said. "How does it feel to be back in yesterday?"

"I'm back in yesterday in more ways than one," Jo replied. "Not so much in Revelstoke, but in Victoria where I grew up. Seeing old friends and familiar places and so forth. It's almost like time-traveling." She took a sip of her chocolate and gazed thoughtfully out the window. Then she turned to Ashley and said, "I'm glad you like the goldstone."

"I wear it every day. Just like you used to."

Jo watched Ashley absentmindedly polishing the goldstone with her fingers. How many dreams has she had? she wondered. Dreams she hasn't remembered? And her reaction by the river, was that a memory that came back without warning? She laughed it off but she must have seen something. It was written all over her face.

"Tell me again how you got it," Ashley said.

"My Aunt Karin left it to me in her will. I was supposed to get it when I turned sixteen, but my grandparents gave it to me early. I was going through a rough time. Your dad might have told you. It was when I suddenly found out we were both adopted. You could say it was a bit of a shock. The goldstone helped a lot. I wore it for years. It was a good luck charm, a family heirloom, a beautiful pendant, all those things. And then I discovered — well, I'd been living in London for about six years and I came home for a visit. My grandma — your great-grandmother — was in the hospital. She noticed I was wearing the goldstone, and she told me something very strange. It was magic, she said. Karin had a way of knowing things because of the goldstone. Because when she wore it to sleep, she could dream the future.

"I don't know if Grandma believed it —"

"Mom and Dad didn't," Ashley interjected. "They laughed when I told them and said I had an overactive imagination, just like you."

"Nothing wrong with that." Jo smiled. "I don't know why Grandma never told me sooner. But that very night, of course, I wanted to try it. So I wore it to sleep and I dreamed about the whales. It didn't seem like much of a future. I tried again a couple of times but the dreams were never what I expected. I started to think, This is ridiculous, I'll carry on and make my own future, same as always. So I stopped dreaming on the goldstone." It wasn't entirely true, but why tell Ashley about a dream she herself didn't understand?

As if reading her thoughts, Ashley said, "Did you ever dream anything scary?"

Jo busied herself with a napkin, wiping water marks off the table, then rearranging the ketchup and vinegar bottles. What should I tell her? That I dreamed about the boy she saw at Rogers Pass, before I knew the goldstone was a magic stone? That I never even remembered the dream until I read her e-mail? Would she laugh it off or take it seriously? Would she be frightened? Or relieved to know she's not alone? Maybe it's nothing. A coincidence. So, again, why worry her unnecessarily? "No," she decided. "Nothing really scary."

"Auntie Jo . . . Am I going to go through a rough time like you did? Is that why you gave me the goldstone?"

Jo reached across the table and squeezed Ashley's hand. "I gave you the goldstone because I wanted you to have it. If I had a daughter I'd give it to her, but since I haven't, you're the next best thing. And since I got it when I was twelve, your twelfth birthday seemed a good time to pass it on. Like a family tradition."

Ashley smiled, pleased with the thought.

It was dark by the time they got home. A fire had been lit in honor of Jo's arrival, and the dining room table was set with special-occasion silver and china. "You want to light the candles, Ashley?" Dad asked. "Dinner will be served shortly. Roast beef and Yorkshire pudding with all the trimmings, and — are you ready for this? A pavlova. Yes, the famous Down Under dessert in honor of our famous guest. So you two better be starving."

Ashley and Jo exchanged guilty looks. At least they'd had a good long walk to build up an appetite.

Later that evening, Ashley had her first taste of champagne.

Dad proposed the toast. "To my famous sister, known to the world as Joanne Gillespie, but to the rest of us as plain old Jo — a late Merry Christmas and Happy New Year and most of all, welcome. We're so glad you're here." Everyone clinked glasses.

Ashley took a sip. The bubbles tickled the inside of her mouth, the back of her throat, and all the way down to her stomach. It's like the taste of laughter, she thought, and happily took another sip.

"Easy now," Mom said. "Don't drink it all at once." She put on a CD and they sat by the fire, listening to the music and sipping champagne.

"Jo, I finally figured out why you've come," Dad said after a while. "It's because of the new adoption laws, isn't it? You've applied to find your birth mother. Or maybe you've already found her?"

Ashley looked at her aunt and wondered what she was going to say. She'd always known about the adoption but it had never concerned her personally. Now it occurred to her that if her aunt *had* found her birth mother, she might also have found another brother. Worse, she might have found another niece to spoil.

"Yes, I know about the new law," Jo said, "but that's not why I came back. I was obsessed for years, wanting to find my birth mother. But not anymore."

Ashley gave a silent sigh of relief.

"I'm still curious," Jo continued. "But the thing is, if I found my birth mother, and father, I'd just be finding my gene pool. That's all. And that's just a part of the person I am. Every experience — it all plays a part in shaping us into who we are. It sometimes takes a long time, but it can be a very fascinating journey."

"Is all this going to end up in your next book?" Ashley wondered.

"Probably! *The Mystery of the Lost Self.* Or something equally profound. Anyway, I think we should drink another toast. To Ashley, who has yet to set off on the journey."

Once again they clinked glasses. Ashley swallowed the tingling sweetness, loving not only the taste of champagne, but the delicious promise of her aunt's words. She was taking her last sip when Jo suddenly leaped up and exclaimed, "Time for more presents!"

She reached over to her bag and pulled out a voluminous garment. "This is for you, Kate," she said, draping it over Mom's shoulders. It was a long felt cape with an Aboriginal design of circles and hand prints and tracks swirling into the large central figure of a kangaroo.

"And Ian, this one's for you." She handed him a vest that appeared to have a thousand and one pockets. "It's for all your bird things. Sunflower seeds and cracked corn and whistles and hooty noise-makers and binoculars and notebooks and pens and whatever else you can think of.

"And Ashley . . . Your mom was telling me about your ski-touring course and that's terrific. But I've got bad news. You won't be doing any of that in Perth. Will she, Kate?"

"Wouldn't think so," Mom said. "What do you think, Ian?"

"Not a chance."

Ashley frowned. "What are you talking about?"

Jo thrust an envelope into her hand. "You can turn it in if you like. I mean, if you'd rather not come."

Ashley tore open the envelope. "What? What is this? A ticket to Australia? Mom, Dad — it's got my name on it! It's a ticket to Perth!" Her voice rose to a delighted shriek. "I don't believe it! Is this for real, Auntie Jo? Fair dinkum? It's really a ticket to Australia? For me?"

"Yes! For you! I'm taking you away from this formidable land of ice and snow and giving you a taste of something completely different. Not forever, just for a month. I'm taking you with me when I go, and your parents'll be coming Down Under to take you back."

"A whole month?" Ashley checked the date. "Leave Vancouver April 24, return on June 6 — it's more than a month! And it's in school time! Ohhh, wait'll I tell Erica!"

As she ran to her room and picked up the phone she couldn't help thinking how wrong her dreams of the future had been. Snow, purple lights, a boy, and a hand. There had never been the slightest hint of Australia.

30

One week later, at the start of spring break, Ashley finally got around to looking through the trunk. Her mother was right. There were several photo albums, and Jo wanted to see them all. Ashley took them out, then decided to dig deeper.

It looked as though the trunk contained nothing but books. There were fairy tales and legends, judging from the covers, many written in what Ashley assumed was Swedish since that was her great-grandparents' native language. There were also books of poetry and an enormous family Bible.

There were household books, stuffed with recipes and all sorts of strange cures. One in particular caught her attention. *To Restore from a Stroke of Lightning. Shower with cold water for two hours; if the patient does not show signs of life, put salt in the water, and continue to shower one hour longer.* She made a mental note to tell Erica in case they got caught in another lightning storm.

She found several sketchbooks near the bottom. The pages were covered with meticulous drawings of wildflowers, neatly labeled and filled in with colored pencils. Ashley recognized most of them from her hikes in the alpine meadows. She knew Mom would be interested and set the books aside.

At the bottom of the trunk she found what appeared to be a diary. It was a thick book, with gilded pages and a cover of reddish-brown leather worn soft by someone's hands. A leather strap with a metal edge enclosed the pages and fitted into a buttoned lock on the front cover. Ashley pushed the button but the strap did not give way. The book was locked.

There had to be a key. Ashley searched the corners of the trunk, then leafed through the pages of every book, thinking a small, thin key might have slipped inside. Nothing. She pulled at the strap, hoping it might be worn enough to come loose. But the strap, and the lock, held firm.

Determined to open it, she went downstairs to her father's workbench and found the snips he used for cutting wire. Then she carefully cut the strap and opened the diary.

She couldn't believe her good fortune. Flowing across the very first page were the words, *The Diary of*

Karin Anderson Warren. Karin! The diary had belonged to her Great-Aunt Karin!

Eagerly she flipped through the pages. Pictures, writing, more pictures . . .

Clearly the sketchbooks had also belonged to Karin. From the looks of things, she'd loved the mountains as much as Ashley did, but there the comparison ended. Ashley couldn't draw a stem, let alone a whole flower.

As for the pictures in the diary, they were mostly of people. And most of them were vaguely familiar. Had she seen them in photographs? That person, for instance, looked like a younger Auntie Jo. About ten years younger, Ashley figured, because there were whales in the sketch. They sprawled across two pages, whales on the beach and whales in the water. And there was the impression of movement — frantic cross-hatchings and shadings, as if Karin had drawn the whales in a hurry, desperate to capture them in her book before they disappeared from her mind.

Ashley smiled, anticipating Dad's reaction when he saw the picture. He'd take it as fresh ammunition for teasing his sister.

Ashley was about to turn the page when it suddenly struck her. Karin had died when Jo was a baby. But somehow she'd known what Jo would look like when she grew up. She'd known about the beach and the stranded whales. She had the goldstone — she must have dreamed about the event, long before it happened. If that was the case, what else had she dreamed?

With growing excitement, Ashley turned to the beginning of the diary. The little boy with the crew cut, that was her dad. She recognized him from old photographs. And there was Jo again. As a young girl, a teenager, an adult. And Dad, grown up, standing by a locomotive. Karin had known he would be an engineer.

And there — no. It couldn't be. But it was. It was Ashley, in her red jacket, standing on the old railway trail at the summit of Rogers Pass.

She felt a sudden chill. Karin had dreamed so far into the future she had dreamed of Ashley. She had even dreamed of the boy. There he was on the opposite page, his face half-masked by falling snow and shadow. Why would Karin have dreamed about him? What was the connection?

Ashley turned the pages slowly, hoping to find some sketches of her future self. Dad and Auntie Jo were shown as children, then adults, so it followed that Karin would have dreamed a grown-up Ashley, too. But there were no more pictures, only words.

Raven would say there was a logical explanation. Either Karin had stopped sketching or Karin had stopped dreaming. As for the other possibility . . .

Ashley shuddered. She didn't dare think of the other possibility.

As soon as she had the chance she would read the diary from cover to cover. The words were bound to reveal more than the pictures.

Ashley and her parents had organized a party that night, a chance for their friends to meet the visiting celebrity. Many of the guests brought copies of Jo's mysteries to be signed, and those who didn't brought autograph books or scraps of paper.

"Can you sign my hand?" Corey asked. "I'm almost in grade two, you know. I read lots of books."

"He just pretends," Jay added. "He can't *really* read that good."

"I've never met a real author before. So can you? Sign my hand?"

"I don't think I better," Jo said. "How about I sign your baseball cap?"

"Sure!" Corey beamed.

After most of the guests had gone home, Jo settled down on the couch with one of the albums Ashley had found in the trunk. "This is the album I remember the best," she said. "Anybody interested? Gather round. We're taking a trip down Memory Lane."

"Is that like Lover's Lane?" Corey asked. "Where the hooked man was?"

"No," said Raven. "It's just a figure of speech."

"What's a figure of speech?"

"Nobody cares," said Jay. "Just look at the pictures."

Every photograph had a story, Jo explained, although she didn't know most of them. She admitted she didn't even know who all the people were, only that the photos had been taken when her grand-parents, the Andersons, were living in the Selkirk Mountains. "The first time I saw these pictures," she said, "they were all jumbled up in a box. I helped my grandma put them into this album."

"Why didn't she tell you who everybody was?" Corey asked.

"She did, but I've forgotten."

"Memory lame," said Raven.

Jo grinned. "*Touché.*"

"What's two shay?" asked Corey.

"It's fake hair," Jay replied in a knowing tone. "What bald people put on their heads."

"That's Glacier House," Ashley's mom said. She pointed to a photo showing three men on a snow-covered roof, two with shovels, one with a saw. A huge block of snow was falling from the roof. "I've seen similar pictures at the museum. They used to saw the snow into blocks, then skid them off the roof."

"Is that your grandad?" Corey pointed to the man with the saw.

"No," Jo said. "Grandad worked for the railway. That's why there's so many pictures of trains."

"That's for sure," Erica remarked. There were trains on trestles, trains in front of stations, trains in the snow.

"Here's a good one," said Jay. He'd flipped back a few pages and found a photo showing a large gathering of people posed around a locomotive. Some stood on the cow-catcher in front, others stood on top behind the smokestack. Everyone was dressed up. Men wore three-piece suits with watch chains looped across their vests. Women wore long dresses and flowery hats. There were several children, too. Small boys in sailor suits, girls wearing high buttoned boots.

Jo pointed to a young girl standing by the locomotive. "That's Karin, the one who grew up and left me the goldstone. And that's her father, my grandfather. And that lady there, that was Grandad's first wife. Karin's mother."

Corey shifted impatiently. "Can we get some more food?" he said. "Then play a game or something?"

"Sure," said Ashley's dad. "There's lots left, everybody. Help yourselves."

They crowded around the buffet table and loaded up their plates while Ashley remained on the couch, looking through the album. So many pictures, so many faces, so many people. All of them gone. All of them ghosts.

She paused at another photograph. This time it showed an older Karin looking directly into the camera with a half-smile on her face, her eyes bright with laughter. And there she was again, slightly older, dressed in a white gown with lace at the throat. It looked like a wedding portrait. Yes, because on the next page she was standing with her handsome groom beside a locomotive decorated with flowers.

Ashley kept looking through the album. There were more photographs of Karin. Alone, with her husband, with family and friends. There she was as an older woman, still fair-haired and beautiful. And in every photo except the first one, even in her wedding portraits, Karin was wearing the goldstone.

"Hey, Ash." Erica plunked down beside her. "We're playing charades. You wanna be on my team?"

"I guess," Ashley said reluctantly. She didn't really

want to play. She wanted everyone to go home, so she could get back to the diary.

31

The house was dark and still when Ashley turned on her lamp, opened Karin's diary, and began to read.

Revelstoke, BC
November 1920
  I have read that "goldstone" is not a stone at all, nor is it any kind of mined mineral. It is made from aventurine glass spangled close and fine with particles of sparkling material like copper shavings or gold flakes. It was first made in monasteries in Italy, a far cry from our Selkirk Mountains. But it came to our mountains nonetheless, and one small goldstone marble somehow found its way into a pedlar's basket. From there it ended up in my mother's hands. And then into mine.

But what of before? Long before the pedlar and his basket, someone created the goldstone. Someone mixed gold and copper into the sand, applied the heat, and shaped the stone. Someone stirred in the magic. How? And why? It doesn't really matter. But Mama was right all those years ago. The goldstone is a magic stone, for dreaming the future.

I have dreamed of the child who will have the goldstone when I am gone. Still further into the future, I have dreamed of a girl named Ashley. Strange name for a girl, Ashley.

Ashley gasped. Karin had not only known what she would look like, she had known her name.

And ever since I moved back to the Selkirks, the dreams have been strange. As if a mysterious force is at work, here in the mountains . . .

What does she mean by that? Ashley read on, hoping to find the answer.

There were several entries spaced out over the next few years, most having to do with the everyday lives of Karin, her family, and friends. One entry was so filled with joy and excitement, Ashley could almost taste the champagne — Karin had sold a series of watercolor paintings to a New York collector who just happened to be hiking in the alpine meadows where Karin had set up her easel.

It wasn't until Ashley reached a much later entry that she found the answer to her question. But not before she read something that made her want to cry.

Revelstoke, BC
August 1936

I dreamed on the goldstone while Stuart was away on his mountain climbing trip. It was too late to warn him. And though I cried out in my sleep and prayed that my thoughts would reach him, it was not to be.

A long time ago, just after the Rogers Pass avalanche, I told Stuart I'd dreamed that I was going to be moving to the coast. Stuart was very upset, and I remember telling him not to worry, that the future was not necessarily carved in stone.

But with the goldstone, what is dreamed cannot be changed. Papa married Lydia and we moved to Victoria on Vancouver Island. Just as the dream foretold. I might have stayed in Victoria, even after I finished high school, if Stuart hadn't lured me back to Revelstoke. But of course I wasn't surprised. I had seen that happy future in a dream.

Now the time for dreaming is over. Stuart's body has been found and will be brought home for burial. I shall bury the goldstone in a manner of speaking, having no desire to dream of a future without my beloved husband.

Revelstoke, BC
September 1938

I was mistaken to think I could simply stop wearing the goldstone. If I don't wear it to bed, I can't sleep. And though the dreams are years away, and largely incomprehensible, they are in many ways becoming clearer. As soon as I wake up I sketch the images revealed the night before. I feel a sense of panic, of urgency, and must get them down!

I dream of events that happen within my family, with Papa, with my five half-sisters and their children, the joys and sorrows that will come to pass. But what to do with this knowledge? After Papa and Lydia were married, I told Lydia they'd have five children, all of them girls. Three first of all, and then after fifteen years, another two. She almost died laughing. By the time she had her last child, she'd no doubt forgotten my words.

According to the Greek legends, Cassandra had the gift of prophecy but she was cursed by never being believed. After Lydia's reaction I stopped saying anything about my dreams. Who would believe me? So now I keep silent, except within the pages of this book.

Revelstoke, BC
January 1942

I am beginning to fade. My energy has gone. I'm only fifty-five, so it cannot be old age. I feel myself growing weaker, as if my energy is crystallizing into the goldstone, as if all my strength is channeled into the dreaming and the compelling urge to capture the dreams on the page. It has become a curse, this goldstone! I don't think it was wise to wear it so often, especially not to sleep, because the more one wears it, the more power it seems to gain.

I haven't written about this before, but here in the mountains I often have the feeling that I'm being watched. When I was a child I felt that the mountains watched over me in a protective sort of way. Strange, for when I consider my experiences with the mountains, "protective" is the last word that comes to mind.

But now the feeling is different. It's an ominous kind of watching. A dark, lurking shadow —

Ashley stopped reading. All she could hear was the thrum of her heart, pounding in her ears.

Karin had felt it, too. The sense of someone watching and waiting. Had she dreamed the boy? Yes, she'd drawn his picture. Did she ever discover the connection?

A dark, lurking shadow creeps around my subconscious and reveals itself in dreams. As soon as I wake up, it's gone. It's like a growing thunderhead. You watch it rise and billow and darken and you wait for the flash of lightning to bring on the storm that will clear the air. But the lightning never comes. The air remains heavy with warning.

I've decided that when I pass on the goldstone, I won't say a word about the dreams. Mama told Papa when she first discovered the magic. He didn't believe her. I told him, too, when I dreamed that the avalanche was coming. He didn't believe me. And later on, neither did Lydia. I'm glad of that now. The secret will die with me.

But I've just written about it, haven't I? I'll have to make sure this diary is destroyed. On the other hand, perhaps I'm worrying needlessly. Who would ever want to read my little diary?

Victoria, BC
March 1946

I moved to Victoria two years ago, to be close to Papa and Lydia. Now that I'm away from the mountains, I no longer experience that ominous feeling I wrote about earlier. Such a relief! The dreams are still as confusing as ever, but there's a recurring dream about snow that I rather like, especially with all the rain we get here. It reminds me a little of home.

The cancer has taken hold — no wonder I was feeling so weak — and I'm in the process of writing my will. I'm leaving the goldstone to my baby niece, Joanne Gillespie, for when she is older. She's the one who will grow up feeling, as I often did, a sense of loss. The goldstone will be a link between us, a talisman to light up that empty space, a connection that says, "We are kindred spirits!" I know this to be true. And so I leave the goldstone to Joanne without disclosing the magic it holds, the magic for dreaming the future.

Ashley reread the last two entries, then closed the diary, her mind reeling. To think that Karin had dreamed the avalanche. To think that all those men had died because she had not been able to warn them. Nor had she been able to stop the avalanche from happening.

Karin was right. It was a curse, dreaming the future. To know what was impossible to change.

32

"Look what I found in the trunk," Ashley said the next morning. She put the diary on the breakfast table and opened it to one of the sketches. "This was Karin's diary and she did all the drawings. Do you recognize this picture, Dad?"

"Sure. It's Jo and me when we were kids. And that's the weeping willow in front of our house." He gave Ashley a puzzled look. "So . . .?"

"So Karin died before you were born. She never saw you as a baby let alone when you were around six, like in this picture. And that's nothing. Auntie Jo, tell Mom and Dad about the whales."

"Well . . ." Jo paused. They hadn't believed Ashley when she told them about the goldstone. Why would they be different now? Was she setting herself up for a new name, Dances with Delusions? Would Ian and Kate be angry with her for drawing Ashley into something that was certainly paranormal, if not potentially dangerous? She looked again at the sketch of her and Ian. The details were uncanny, right down to her ponytail.

"Come on, Jo," Dad urged. "I can't imagine there's anything you *haven't* told us about the whales, but let's hear it."

She decided to plunge right in. "The last time I saw Grandma, she told me the goldstone was magic, and that I could dream the future."

"You've got to be kidding!" Dad laughed. "Grandma was in on this, too?"

"Just listen!" And she proceeded to describe her dream about the whales.

After Jo finished, Ashley turned to the corresponding sketch in Karin's diary. "See? Karin dreamed this, too! And there's way more." She turned the pages slowly, letting them look at each picture in turn. Finally she came to the last sketch, the one that showed her and the boy on the old railway trail.

"Good grief." Dad stared at the drawing, all laughter gone from his face. "That looks like — I can't make out the face, but the clothes, the way he's standing — that looks like the kid Raven and I saw, the time we went birding."

"You won't believe this," Jo said quietly. "But I've seen him, too."

"Where, here in town?" said Mom.

"No, it was at the summit of Rogers Pass. Over thirty years ago. Ian, you remember that trip we went on with Mom and Dad, the summer the Rogers Pass highway opened?"

He nodded. "It was just before you started university. We went to the Rockies and stayed in Banff. It was a great trip."

"Well, if you remember, we stopped at the summit to take pictures and after we left I fell asleep in the car. I was wearing the goldstone —"

"As always."

"And I had a dream. I didn't think anything of it at the time. And don't forget, this happened long before I knew the goldstone was magic. But you know what dreams are like. They're jumbled and they don't make sense and they're always full of people you don't know or recognize and they're doing all sorts of crazy or interesting or adventurous things. I always wonder what I end up doing in other peoples' dreams. Don't you ever wonder —"

"Jo, stop rambling."

"Sorry." She let out her breath in one long sigh, then shifted her attention to Ashley. "The dream I had in the car that day, I forgot it as soon as I woke up. It was your e-mail that brought it back, when you told me about the boy you saw at the summit. As soon as I read it, I knew it was the same boy. And seeing Karin's drawing . . . " She shook her head in amazement. "And there was something else in the dream. Something to do with snow, and the feeling that I had to get Ashley away."

"Oh, come on!" Ashley gave a dismissive laugh and tried to ignore the sense of foreboding that welled up in her chest. "You came to do book signings and to see us." She remembered what her aunt had said about the whales, how they came together when one was stranded. Well, that wasn't Ashley. She was hardly in danger.

She looked at her mom, her dad, and her aunt, all gazing at her with worried and anxious expressions. "Stop staring at me! There's a rational explanation. I'll tell Raven, he'll figure it out. What am I supposed to do, sit at home forever? Anyway, I'm going to Australia pretty soon so you won't have to worry about me and the snow."

Mom frowned. "I'm not sure about this snow. Maybe you better not go on that ski-touring trip tomorrow."

"Mo-om! I've been looking forward to it for weeks! It's not like I haven't been skiing practically every day for months!"

Mom glanced over at Dad. "What are the conditions at Glacier?"

"They're . . . good. I checked this morning. Stable snow, avalanches unlikely, backcountry travel generally safe."

"See, Mom? And there's still snow in town. How can I avoid the snow? There's no escape!"

Mom gave a small smile. "You've got a point. If the conditions . . . if your dad . . ." She looked at him expectantly.

"I'll double check first thing tomorrow," he said, "but it's supposed to be good all week. And it's not like she's going alone. Matt Godfrey's an excellent guide. I think —"

"No!" Jo exclaimed. "I don't think . . ." Her voice trailed off. She thought of her last dream on the goldstone and how disturbing it was. But how could she articulate her worries when she couldn't even remember the wretched dream? Everyone was looking at her. The last thing they needed was some interfering relative spreading doom and gloom. The diary was bad enough. "Sorry. What do I know? You're the parents. You're the ski experts."

She wouldn't say another word. Today was Sunday. She'd wait until tomorrow, then see about changing the tickets. She'd leave for Australia earlier than planned and take Ashley away from the snow.

Ashley spent the rest of the day wishing she had never shown the others the diary. She took it away and stashed it at the bottom of her messiest drawer. She didn't want them poring over the pictures, reading the text, and jumping to a million conclusions. They'd already seen enough to start the worry wheels turning.

Of course she knew *why* she had shown them. She'd hoped they'd dismiss it as nonsense, not take Karin's words and pictures seriously. As for Dad recognizing the boy and Auntie Jo's dream — that was a total shock.

Well, she wouldn't show them she was afraid. Besides, what could she do about it? Karin had dreamed the avalanche but what good did that do?

Everyone got buried. The fact that Ashley's great-grandfather missed it was a fluke. It had nothing to do with Karin's dream.

Ashley dreamed on the goldstone that night, the first time she'd done so in ages, hoping for a glimpse of Australia or something that would assure her she *did* have a future beyond Karin's last sketch. But the dream contained all the images she'd seen before — the boy, the hand, and the snow. And in the morning, as she was getting ready for the ski trip, she remembered two other elements. There was a cabin. An old log cabin half-buried in snow, its moss-covered roof sagging precariously, its open door falling off the hinges.

And there was something else, something blue against the snow. Not an ordinary blue, but a vivid, almost dark-turquoise blue.

"Have you got enough layers on?" Mom asked when Ashley was ready to leave. "Are you sure your red jacket's warm enough? It's still cold up there."

"Mo-om! Stop fussing! I've been wearing this jacket all winter."

"The forecast's great," Dad said. "You've got a perfect day."

"Good!" Ashley smiled and gave herself a mental pat on the back. Worried about a dream? Meet it head on. Touring in Glacier National Park? Of course there'd be snow. So what? There'd been snow since October. And the avalanche danger was low.

As for the cabin? There were plenty of alpine cabins

in the park. Some old, some new. So what? She wasn't going to be alone. And if she happened to see a dilapidated cabin with an open door, she wouldn't go inside. Simple! A cabin wasn't going to reach out and grab her.

As for that strange turquoise blue? Maybe it was the mountain bluebird she'd dreamed about before. But it was the wrong season and they were uncommon at the best of times. She chased the image away.

"You sure you're going to be all right?" Auntie Jo asked. "I know you're a terrific skier and everything . . ."

"I'll be fine!" Ashley gave her aunt a hug. "But thanks for worrying. And I promise I won't go near the cabin."

She was halfway out the door when she heard Mom say, "What's she talking about now? Who said anything about a cabin?"

33

Time, as Jonathan had known it, no longer existed.

There were no days or weeks or hours, no sunrise or sunset, no darkness, no light.

He shimmered in a pale purple glow, looking out from within at a world that was slowly fading away.

He no longer knew time, but knew that the time of the dream was drawing near.

Soon he would keep his promise.

Soon he would be able to sleep.

34

Mr. Godfrey, the leader of the ski-touring trip, was counting heads as the fifteen skiers got into the minibus. "Safety first," he said. "And we'll all stay together."

"Didn't know it was Godfrey leading the group," Raven muttered. "If I'd known it was Godfrey, I never would've come. What happened to Vic? He was the one teaching the course."

"Dad said he got sick," Ashley said, "so Mr. Godfrey took his place."

"You knew and didn't tell me?"

"What difference does it make?"

"You know I can't stand Godfrey. He hates me! You should've said something."

"What's the problem? He's not your teacher anymore. Just make the best of it."

It wasn't long before they reached a plowed parking area alongside the highway, a mile or so west of the Rogers Pass summit. Mr. Godfrey parked the minibus and everyone tumbled out. "Make sure your packs are in order," he said. "You all got the list of suggestions for lunch and snacks. Remember, if you can't fall on it, leave it behind. Check your ski equipment, let me know if you need any help with your bindings. And get your skins on. They'll make the climbs much safer. You might want to leave them on when you're skiing downhill, too, especially if you've got a heavy pack. They'll help reduce the speed."

Raven looked up from applying his skins and rolled his eyes. "We know what to do. We took the course."

"Just a reminder," Mr. Godfrey said pleasantly. "And there are a few who don't have quite your level of expertise."

"Shouldn't be allowed to come then," Raven grumbled.

"What's that?"

"Nothing. Can't we just go?"

"When we're ready." Mr. Godfrey turned to the rest of the group. "Everyone listening? Erica, Raven? Could I have your attention, too, please? Thank you. All right, everyone. Here's the plan. Once we leave the parking lot we'll head west and climb a hill above the highway until we get to an old road. Then we'll follow the road and the old railway grade back to the left aways —"

"Blah, blah, blah."

"Speak up, Raven, if you've got something to add."

"I was just saying, then we pass a monument and the junction and there's a trail on the right where all the ski tours start. I've been there a million times."

"Good. I'm sure you'll be a big help. Now as I was about to say, there's usually old ski tracks to show the way, but I want you all to follow me. You, too, Raven. No dashing ahead or going off on your own."

"When's lunch?" Scout asked.

"Whenever we get to the hut," Mr. Godfrey replied. "A couple of hours at the most."

Raven glanced at the group, some of whom were still adjusting their packs. "A couple of hours? Try midnight tomorrow. I thought this was supposed to be the advanced group. Hey, Mr. Godfrey? Isn't that what the notice said?"

"It did and it is. No one here's a beginner. And no one's forcing you to come. You can wait right here if you like."

"Nah, that's OK. Can we go now?"

"All in good time. First we'll do some easy flat skiing to stretch our muscles before we start to climb. And a few tips — Raven, boys, are you listening? Remember to keep your heads up. Don't stare at your ski tips. And remember that climbing's hard work, so just use the muscles you need to use and relax everything else. And don't forget to breathe! Sometimes if you get nervous or anxious you hold your breath without meaning to. Don't! Breathe fear out and power in. And if you fall, don't get upset, just laugh it off."

Raven laughed lightly. "Can we go *now*?"

"Yup, it looks like we're all set. Raven, you can help by staying at the end of the line. Make sure there aren't any stragglers. OK, group. Fall in!"

"Wagons ho!" Raven shouted. "Yee-ha!"

Push off and glide . . . Rollerblading with a pack on was how Ashley described the motion. She loved the feel of gliding across the snow, the swishing sound of the skis, the satisfying squeak of the bindings, the stillness of the mountains. She loved the exhilarating rush of downhill skiing, but touring gave her the time to contemplate the scene instead of whizzing through it. And in the backcountry, it was never crowded.

Push off and glide . . . Imagine gripping the snow with your toes. That's what Dad had told her. Then follow with a push from the heel that rolls off the big toe as the leg passes behind. Transfer your weight from the pushing leg to the forward leg. Get into a rhythm, your own diagonal stride. Push off and glide . . .

It was a perfect day. The snow sparkled in the sun. There wasn't a breath of wind. Even so, it was cold, and Ashley was glad of her long, thermal underwear.

When they reached the first hill Mr. Godfrey stopped everyone and gave more instructions. "If you need to rest on the way up, make sure you put your skis *across* the slope and stomp out a good platform. If you stop with your skis facing *up* the hill, you could slip backward."

Raven gave a loud snort of laughter. "That's pretty obvious, isn't it? Who'd be that stupid?"

Mr. Godfrey glared at Raven but otherwise ignored the interruption. "Climbing can be tough, as I said before. But keep a positive attitude and go at your own pace. And don't worry if you can't keep up with everyone else. We'll wait for you if you fall behind. Just clear your mind, find your own rhythm, and enjoy the day."

"Forever," Raven muttered. "We have to wait for all the laggers? This day'll last for-flipping-ever." He continued to mutter as they climbed the hill.

Ashley couldn't make out his exact words, but wished he'd shut up. Talk about a waste of energy. He was probably reciting some trivia about snowflakes or touring equipment. Or planning new ways to torment Mr. Godfrey.

More likely, he was sticking verbal daggers into his dad's girlfriend. Ashley knew that's what was really bothering him. He'd been bad enough in the fall when he first met Misty Whatever. But since Christmas, when his dad announced they were going to be married — and were expecting a baby — Raven had been impossible.

His attitude became even more annoying during the lunch break. Ashley had no sooner finished her cheese sandwich and second power bar when he started in. "Hey, Mr. Godfrey? Did you know that Ottawa is the second coldest national capital in the world? And the coldest is Ulaanbaatar? That's in Mongolia. And it's so cold there your breath turns to ice crystals. They call it the whispering of the stars. Did you know that?"

"Hmmm . . ."

"I'm just telling you, that's all. You'd think a teacher would be interested."

Even when Mr. Godfrey made a deliberate point of turning his back, Raven wouldn't let up. "After lunch can we take that trail we passed back there? Hey, Mr. Godfrey?"

"No, I've told you before. We're staying on this trail."

"Ahh . . . Can't we go any faster, then? This whole trip sucks!"

"Then go back to the parking lot!" Mr. Godfrey spun around angrily. "I've had enough of your complaining! Go on, pick up your backpack and go! I'll expect to find you there when we get back."

"How can I? You said we couldn't go off on our own. Didn't he, Erica? You heard him. That's what he said."

Mr. Godfrey put on his backpack and motioned for the others to get ready. Then he turned to Raven and said, "This is the last trip you're coming on. Trust me, your father's going to hear about this."

"My father?" Raven sneered. "That's a good one. C'mon, Scout. Clipper. Let's bring up the rear."

Ashley skied over to Raven as they were starting out. "Why don't you smarten up?" she said. "Nobody's the least bit impressed. You're making everybody miserable."

"You'd know about that, wouldn't you, Ashley? How to make a person miserable."

Erica, standing close by, gave a dry laugh. "That's for sure."

Ashley's stomach turned cold. Those hurtful words she'd flung at Raven, the way she'd blamed Erica . . . It was so long ago she'd almost forgotten. She'd assumed the others had, too.

Obviously they hadn't. And from the looks that were passing between Raven and Erica, the missing-goldstone incident had done more than set Ashley apart.

She felt a pang of loneliness, worse than any twinge of jealousy. It wasn't that she had a crush on Raven, although that notion had once, fleetingly, crossed her mind. It was the possibility that she might once again lose her two best friends.

They skied on in silence, through a stand of hemlock, then across an open meadow. When Mr. Godfrey and the first half of the group went around a curve and out of sight, Raven called out to his friends, "Wait up, you guys! Stop for a sec."

"What's the matter?" asked Clipper.

Raven pointed. "See that slope? Just over the other side there's a lake."

"So?" The girls gave him a puzzled look.

"I was just thinking . . . Yeah. I'm going to do it."

"Do what?" Ashley said.

"Ski over to the lake. That's where I went with your dad that time. I'm sure it's the same place."

"You can't leave the group," she said. "You have to stay with everybody else."

Raven's mouth tightened. "I'm sick of everybody else. And Godfrey barking orders every two seconds. Stay together. Not so fast. Blah, blah, blah. Come on, it'll be cool. We'll climb up that slope, check out the other side, then ski back to the trailhead. We'll probably get there before Godfrey. OK?"

Ashley shook her head. "I don't think so. Mr. Godfrey said —"

"Jeez, Ashley! What's he gonna do, ground you? He's not your teacher. You're not in school. Why're you acting like such a wimp all of a sudden?" He turned to the others. "How about it, you guys? You can ski as good as me. Maybe better, eh, Scout? C'mon, it'll be an adventure."

He waited for a moment while they argued amongst themselves, then turned and set out across the snow.

Ashley wasn't surprised when Erica followed. "Wait for me!" she cried. "I'm coming!"

Clipper was next. "Oh, what the heck. C'mon, Scout." The boys took off after Erica.

Steph drummed her fingers on her ski poles. "Well, Ashley? Whaddya think?"

"Go ahead. You hardly need my permission." Ashley smiled to show there were no hard feelings, and watched Steph ski after the others.

They made their way up the slope, Erica and Raven in the lead, talking and laughing together. Once again Ashley felt left out and stranded. I'm like Auntie Jo's whales after all, she thought ruefully. Only instead of joining me, the others are moving away.

"Come on, Ash!" Erica called from her resting platform, halfway up the slope.

Ashley examined her options. At least this time she had a choice. She could ski after Mr. Godfrey and the others. Or she could wait. Eventually Mr. Godfrey would realize he was missing half the group, and he'd come back to round them up. If he wasn't doing so already.

She could go back to the parking lot by herself, although she didn't relish that option. She'd lost track of how far they'd come and wasn't sure if she could find her way back down. Raven was the one who knew. He was the one who'd spent hours touring with her dad, way more than she ever had.

It wasn't too late to go back. She could probably find her way by following their ski tracks. But what if other skiers were in the area making different tracks? It could be confusing. And it wasn't wise to be out alone, not in the backcountry.

The others had now reached the top of the slope. "Hurry up!" Erica shouted. "We're going on ahead!"

Ashley waved up at her friends. And made her decision.

35

High on the slope, Jonathan was watching.

He knew that on the peaks of the mountains, millions of tons of ice and snow hung poised. Avalanches waiting to happen.

He knew an avalanche wasn't likely. Not now, not when it hadn't snowed for almost a month. That was the most dangerous time, during or after a heavy snowfall.

If the snow was unstable, anything could trigger an avalanche. A mountain goat crossing a gully. Sunshine warming a snow-covered hill. A lone skier crossing a hillside. Even experts could be caught by surprise.

As for the young people climbing the slope? They were not experts. And they were far too noisy. Loud voices, raucous laughter — their noise broke the hush of the mountains and shattered the awesome silence.

Five together, one alone. They looked garish in their bright clothing. Red, blue, yellow, purple, shades he had never seen on people, not when he was young.

And the clothing and skis were noisy. Every movement of arm and leg made a rustle, a crackle, a swish, a creak.

Be still! he wanted to shout. But he held back, knowing the five noisy ones had to cross the slope. They had to leave the other one behind.

He knew it was her. He had dreamed this very scene. The splashes of color, like wildflowers scattered over the snow. And standing alone, one red columbine. The Ashley.

In his dream, a raven had shown him the way. But that wasn't right. There was no sign of a raven. Unless — unless the raven was yet to come? Perhaps he should wait.

No, he'd waited long enough. The time was right. The place was right. He had found the Ashley girl. He knew she had the goldstone. It was almost within his grasp.

He moved toward the jagged peaks of the mountain where a gentle slope became a steeper hillside. Here, the snow had piled up. Layer upon layer, week after week, month after month, each new layer binding itself to the layers already anchored to the mountainside.

Hidden underneath was another layer. A layer made slippery by the melting snow that seeped down through the surface.

Jonathan knew what to do. With one bold stroke, he shimmered his hand across the snow.

A crack shot over the surface.

The snow began to slide.

36

Ashley didn't want to be alone.

It was too much like the last time, watching her friends from the outside, wishing she could join in.

"Wait!" she yelled and headed toward the slope. She hadn't gone more than a few feet when she felt a sudden, unexpected wind. At the same time, she heard a rumbling, like thunder rolling deep underground.

The others started screaming, "Ashley, get outta there! Go, go!"

Dry, powdery crystals jumped in the wind. Above her, the snow was a white wave, sliding, streaming, roaring down the mountain at over one hundred miles an hour.

Ashley stood frozen in its path.

"Ski to the side! Go, go, go!"

She made herself lunge across the snow, her heart pounding with terror. Could she make it? What if she couldn't? If she was caught —

In that instant, she knew she didn't have a chance. She threw down her poles, kicked off her skis, and dropped her pack. She was in the act of flinging herself to the side when the avalanche hit.

It lifted her like a rag doll and hurled her into the boiling fury of the wave. Knee deep, waist deep, chest deep. Feet gone, sky gone, head over heels, a twisting whirl of white, only inside it was spinning utter darkness.

Hold your breath! Don't open your mouth!

The wave tossed her from darkness to light, to air and to sunlight, but she couldn't stop rolling, she couldn't get out, she couldn't take more than a gasp, a breath, before being rolled back down into the dark.

She swam with the wave, pulling and kicking with arms and legs, fighting to get back to the top, but the force was too great, the tide too strong. She grabbed at her face and rolled with the wave, doubled up and stretched out, snapped and stretched, she rolled and rolled and rolled.

Finally she felt the slowing down. The stillness. The crushing weight of snow.

37

Raven had known what was coming the instant he'd felt the wind and heard the snap of trees.

First, the flurry.

Then, the avalanche.

He'd screamed Ashley's name. He'd seen her move, drop the poles, stumble out of her skis, and throw herself toward the side. And he'd seen her disappear in the tidal wave of snow.

Now the avalanche had settled, and Raven was so overwhelmed he scarcely knew where to begin. Ashley was buried, they had to get her out. But how? When? What if they couldn't find her?

Stop! he told himself. Stop and think! He had to do something. He didn't want to, he wanted somebody else to take charge. Mr. Godfrey, anybody. He wanted to turn back time, to be safe with the group, to hear Ashley telling him to smarten up. He wanted one of the others to make a decision, to say what had to be done, but they were too stunned. Erica was so white he thought she would faint for real. Steph was making whimpering sounds and clawing at the sleeves of her jacket. Clipper and Scout were speechless, their faces gray and pinched with shock.

So Raven took charge. "Come on, you guys!" he shouted.

His words spurred the others into action, and they followed him down the slope. "We've gotta get help!" Erica wailed. "What are you doing, we've gotta get help!"

"There isn't time!" Raven cried. "We've got to find her ourselves."

He knew about avalanches. He'd taken a course on avalanche safety. He'd done a report. *In 1962 an avalanche fell from the highest mountain in Peru. It covered ten miles in fifteen minutes. It destroyed six villages and killed over 3,500 people. In 1981 an enormous slab avalanche fell from Mount Sanford, Alaska. It traveled eight miles before stopping. It carried enough ice and snow to fill all the boxcars in a sixty-mile-long train.*

All the avalanche trivia Raven had ever collected raced through his mind as he skied to the end of the run-off zone. All the fascinating facts. Like brain damage occurs about four minutes after the brain is deprived of oxygen. And after ten minutes, survival is unlikely even if breathing is restored. And few people survive if they're buried more than six feet deep. Unless they're lucky enough to have a breathing space in front of their faces. A large breathing space.

And when an avalanche races down a hillside, there's a lot of air mixed in with the moving snow. But as soon as the avalanche stops, the snow crystals pack tightly together. The air is forced out. The snow becomes hard. People buried cannot move their arms or legs.

Raven knew all this. He knew they'd have to probe. If she wasn't buried too deep, they had a 70 percent chance of finding her. They'd have to use ski poles, and they were only good for about three feet. If she was deeper than that . . .

How much time did they have? Not much. Even if she did have a large breathing space, if they didn't find her within an hour, her chances of surviving were down to 30 percent. Another fascinating bit of trivia. Hardly trivial. Hardly fascinating. Now the knowledge was deadly.

"Anybody see anything?" he shouted. "A mitt or hat or something?"

They scanned the avalanche path, hoping for a sign, a clue, anything that might indicate she was buried near the surface.

Nothing.

They agreed on the spot where Ashley had last been seen and marked it with a ski. At least they wouldn't have to search above that point. And at least this avalanche had slowed down and stopped on level ground. It hadn't fallen into a deep gully or ravine. Even so, the area they had to search was immense. Snow was piled some twenty feet deep. And somewhere inside was Ashley.

Erica was hysterical. "We should have worn those beacon things, I told you we should've, if we had beacons we could hear her and know where she was but now we'll never find her, we'll never —"

"Shut up!" Raven hurriedly took a knife from his pack and cut the basket off his ski pole. Then he handed the knife to the others so they could do the same. "We have to probe."

"First we've gotta get organized," Scout said shakily. "Get in a line. I saw it on TV. You stand with your hands on your hips, elbow to elbow so you don't miss a spot. That's the proper spacing."

Raven pointed to the right edge of the slide. "She started to go in this direction, so we better start on this side. Steph, put one of your skis over there, to mark the left-side boundary. So we can keep track of where we're going . . . In case we have to do a second probe, farther along . . . And a third . . ." He blinked hard and forced himself to concentrate on *now*.

They formed a line at the toe of the slide, then inserted their ski poles in the space between their feet. Down, then up. They moved forward one step and probed again. Forward and probe, advancing up the slope.

It wasn't long before they got into a rhythm.

Pull up, move forward, probe down.

Up . . . forward . . . down.

Each time they left something to mark the row. A ski. A mitt. A candy wrapper.

Thank goodness there were five of them. Any fewer and they would hardly make a dent in the width of the slide. They hardly made a dent as it was.

Up . . . forward . . . down.

Each time hoping the pole would touch Ashley. They'd have no doubt about the contact. A rock or tree stump wouldn't give like a body.

Up . . . forward . . . down.

Everyone was silent. Straining to hear the slightest sound that might reveal Ashley's location.

Up . . . forward . . . down.

Raven wished they could go faster. Probing wasn't the best way to search for someone, but right now it was the only way they had. Speed was important but they couldn't go tearing around in a panic. Like Scout said, they had to be organized.

Erica was talking under her breath. "We shouldn't've come, we should've stayed with the others. Where are they now, back at the trailhead? Or at the parking lot? Maybe they've gone back to the hut. They'll look for us, won't they? Won't they? They'll wonder if — oh, Ashley, I'm sorry, I should've stayed with you, I should've . . ."

Shut up! Raven wanted to scream. Instead, he said quietly, "We'll find her, Erica. You're doing great."

She pulled up her pole, stepped forward in the line, probed down again. Her face was taut with fear.

They all felt it, the numbing fear. The panic. As for Ashley, Raven couldn't begin to imagine how she must be feeling. And the other possibility, that she was beyond feeling? He pushed that thought from his mind.

38

Was she alive?

Ashley had come to rest with her arms bent and her hands cupped around her face, just enough to create a small pocket of air. She could breathe. If she took shallow, shallow breaths, she could breathe.

She couldn't move.

Her heart raced, a rapid, uneven fluttering that made her sick with panic. She was so tightly packed in by snow she couldn't move, couldn't cry, couldn't scream . . .

Stay calm. Stay calm.

Which way was up? She put out her tongue and licked at the snow, licked enough to swallow, to see if it went down to her stomach. It did. *Up* was above her head, then. But how far above?

Where are the others? she cried silently. Are they up there now, digging me out? Did they see where I landed? How far away were they, how far, and how long can I stay buried before —?

Stay calm.

What if they're still mad? For what I did, for what I said? What if they haven't forgiven me? What if they, if they go away and leave me —?

Stay calm. They'll find you. They were there, they saw it happen. *Stay calm.*

Breathing was difficult. If she moved her hand, tried to push some of the snow away . . .

Oh, God, no! The air space disappeared. Snow fell in and choked her, made her gasp and cough.

Stay calm. Don't struggle.

Slowly, with her fingers, she carved out a tiny space around her nose. She could breathe. She found her rhythm and listened to the voice inside her head.

Breathe in. Breathe out. Power in. Fear out. Hope in. Fear out.

Don't think of the dark.

Don't think of the cold.

Think of the goldstone, a sun at your throat. Warmth in, cold out. Warmth to your heart, warmth to your belly, warmth to your fingertips, through to your toes. Hope in, fear out. Warmth in, cold out.

A deeper darkness began to close in. She didn't fight it, but held on to her breath, the only sound in the deadening silence, faint as the whispering of the stars. Who said that, about the whispering . . . ? *Warmth in, gold out, light in, dark out, white in, black out . . .*

Then she heard the voice in her head saying, *Look, Ashley. There's a light. Someone's calling your name.*

"Ashhh-ley . . ."

Hear that? And look, there's a hand reaching in. Take it. Take the hand. Follow the light.

39

The silence was tangible.

Where are the others? Ashley wondered. It was strange she couldn't see them. Had they been buried, too?

And where had the boy come from? She hadn't seen him earlier, although she'd certainly seen him before. She recognized him the moment he brought her out of the darkness. He was the boy from the abandoned railway trail. The boy she had dreamed. She didn't know why she'd been frightened. He seemed perfectly nice. And how lucky he'd come along when he did. But why was he leading her up the mountain instead of down?

She was curious, not worried. After all, she could breathe. She was free.

She found it surprisingly easy to move through the deep snow, even without her skis. Almost as if her body was floating. No, it was as if she'd left her body behind. Even more surprising was the fact that the boy she was following did not leave any footprints. If he vanished like before, she'd have no tracks to follow.

Better keep up then. She opened her mouth to tell the boy to slow down but the words wouldn't come.

Breathe in. Breathe out. Breathing was still difficult. Speaking was impossible. Better keep following. Perhaps the boy knew a quicker way down the mountain.

She almost laughed. Going up was hardly a quicker way to go down.

As if he sensed her discomfort, the boy turned around and said, "It's not much farther."

Ashley could hear his words, unlike the first time she'd encountered him. Good! When they got to wherever they were going, he'd have some explaining to do.

She saw a light in the distance, shining at the edge of the snowfield. It was a strange light, with tinges of pink and blue. Not sunlight or moonlight, but something else. A light that washed the snow an eerie shade of purple.

As she drew closer she noticed the cabin, half hidden in the snow drifts, but lit by the same purple glow. It looked abandoned, although the path to the doorway was clear.

"Follow me," said the boy. He led her down the path to the open door.

Ashley paused for a moment, feeling a vaguely remembered tug. Go or stay? Before she could decide, the boy beckoned. And Ashley found herself drifting inside.

40

Ashley's father was lost in a book when Jo rushed into the room, her face a mixture of fear and alarm. "Ian!" she cried. "You've got to go and stop her!"

He looked up from his book and said patiently, "We've already discussed this, Jo. I'm sure Ashley —"

"You don't understand," Jo rushed on. "It's the cabin, what she said about the cabin. Look, just before I sent her the goldstone I had one last dream. I woke up terrified, my heart was pounding. I couldn't remember a thing about it until now. Ian, I was walking by the river, thinking about Ashley — and it all came back. 'I won't go near the cabin!' That's what she said when she left this morning. But the thing is —

she's not going to have a choice. She's going to be trapped. She'll never get out."

"Jo, you're getting yourself all worked up —"

"Pay attention!" she shouted. "Aren't you listening? It's my fault! I never would've sent her that goldstone if I'd known. Never! The night I had that dream, I thought it was just me, some kind of mid-life panic attack —" She stopped abruptly, took several deep breaths, and forced herself to calm down. Then, in a lower voice, she said, "I know it's insane. I don't have any details, I don't have a clue what this is all about. So just humor me. Just go. You know where she's skiing, you're an expert in the backcountry. Please." Her face crumpled. "If anything happens . . ."

"Sure, Jo." He put his arms around her. "You want to come? Or wait here and tell Kate? She'll be home around two."

"I'll stay." She made an attempt to smile. "Don't want to slow you down."

He quickly changed his clothes and loaded his gear in the car. As a second thought, he went back inside and filled a thermos with hot chocolate. Ashley probably wouldn't need it, but it would hit the spot.

41

Once upon a time, someone had lived in the cabin. Threads of cloth hung in tatters at the broken windows. Half the roof had collapsed, and one wall looked as though it were about to fall down. Snowdrifts covered the wood stove and the pile of firewood stacked beside it.

Oil lamps, their soot-blackened chimneys partially hidden by a veil of snow, stood on counters and on the rough wooden table. Two bunks leaned against one wall, but mice and other small animals had burrowed into the mattresses and made nests out of the blankets and quilt batting.

Dishes and cooking utensils lay in a snowy clutter along one shelf, and tin cans lined another. The cans were rusted with age, their labels blackened with mildew or peeling from the damp.

The open shelves on the opposite wall held an assortment of clear glass jars. Some were filled with flakes of copper and gold, so fine they looked like grains of sand. Others contained pieces of broken glass — red, orange, brown, amber — glinting in the purple light.

The boy followed her gaze. "Most of the glass is in the shed," he said. "Or was, until the storms tore it down. Now it's all buried in snow. But it comes back in the spring melt. You'll see."

How will I see? Ashley wondered.

The boy smiled. "I'm glad you're here. There was supposed to be a raven to show the way, and I waited and waited. I didn't see any birds today, but it doesn't matter, does it? You're here." He sat on one of the two ladder-back chairs propped up against the snow-covered table and motioned for her to do the same.

Ashley sat as directed. The snow clung to her fingers when she placed her hand on the table, and as she shook it off, she wondered what had happened to her mitts. She noticed the gloves the boy was wearing, how they were worn through at the fingertips. Smooth and cold, that's how the glove had felt when she'd held on to it. Smooth and cold and light, as if it were empty.

But, of course, it wasn't empty. His hand had pulled her to safety. His hand was a lifeline.

Breathe in. Breathe out. Could she speak? Or would she be wasting her breath? If she formed the words in her mind and uttered them slowly and calmly . . . She tried. "Do you live here?"

"I used to," the boy replied. "When I was young. A long time ago."

"Couldn't be. That long ago." She spoke in short, measured phrases, taking a long breath between each one. "You don't look. Very old."

"Don't I?" He smiled. "Guess how old I am."

His words had a familiar ring. I'm in a fairy tale, Ashley thought. Rumplestiltskin. Except instead of guessing his name, I have to guess his age. If I get that right, he'll let me go. But why would I think that? I'm not a prisoner.

"Give up?" He smiled again, looking very pleased with himself. "I'll give you a clue. I'm older than your goldstone."

Breathe in. Breathe out. Power in. Fear out. "How did you know? About the goldstone?"

"Can I see it?"

She nodded. With fumbling fingers she unfastened the top of her jacket and loosened the pendant from the folds of her sweater.

The boy leaned forward for a closer look. "That's the one," he said excitedly. "And this is the other one." He reached into his shirt pocket and drew out a second goldstone, the same size but darker than the first. He held it out to Ashley, and in that moment it struck her. The jars of gold flakes, the pieces of glass —

"You! You made. The goldstones."

He nodded proudly. "After the lightning. After I became Grandfather's right hand. I made hundreds, souvenirs for the tourists. Grandfather taught me. He made the one you've got. And mine. They're not ordinary goldstones, they're special. They're lightning stones, from the spirits of Avalanche Mountain.

"That one you're wearing, it got mixed up with the others after the lightning. It got mixed up, and I took it to the pedlar. It disappeared. I promised Grandfather I'd find it and bring it back. He's gone now, gone to sleep by the Glacier. But I mean to keep my promise.

"I know you're the Ashley girl. I saw you in my dreams. It was because of you I left the mountain and signed on with the railway. It was because of you I was buried alive by the avalanche."

"What? What avalanche?"

"The one in Rogers Pass. The one from Avalanche Mountain."

Ashley stared at the boy, stunned. Avalanche Mountain — he means the one Karin dreamed and couldn't prevent. The one my great-grandfather — and this boy was there. He didn't escape. He was buried.

"No one knew who I was," the boy continued, "because I didn't sign on. They wrote down what I looked like, what I was wearing, what I had with me. One red marble, that's what they called my goldstone. Nobody knew who I was. So they called me Unknown. That's what they carved on the gravestone. Unknown. I can't read it myself, but that's what I heard them say."

He paused and tilted his head, as if listening to someone. Then he looked at Ashley and said, "You'll have to give me the goldstone. I can't touch it because I'm not real. When you join me in the ether world, when you begin to shimmer, then I'll be able to touch it. I've waited for so long, almost one hundred years."

Ashley didn't think she'd heard correctly. Surely he meant *other* world, not ether world. And what did he mean by that? What did he mean by shimmer? He must have meant shiver.

He reached out an arm, and she felt the dank, stone cold of something buried deep in the ground. "It was you," she said. "That night. In my room."

The boy nodded proudly. "I almost had the goldstone that time, but it wasn't the right place. This is the place. This has always been the place. In the mountains. In the snow. I know from the dreams."

"Yes . . ." Ashley whispered. She was terribly cold. And so tired. Every breath took forever. All she wanted to do was sleep. But something told her she had to stay awake.

Questions. She had to ask questions, keep him talking until she was found. Ask how he made the goldstones. What his grandfather was like. How they'd managed to live so far from town. Wasn't he lonely? What did he mean by the lightning?

One by one he answered her questions. He told her about his grandfather and their treks to the village, about the fire and the ice, about the giant spark that split the sky and changed their lives forever.

Ashley listened with a mixture of fascination and terror. Something was happening, something beyond the boy's words and the cold, strangely lit cabin. Her hand, the hand that still clasped the goldstone at her throat, was beginning to glow. She could scarcely feel a heartbeat. She was slipping deeper into the dream.

Then she noticed that the boy had stopped talking and was staring at her intensely. Had his eyes always been such a startling shade of blue? She'd seen the color before, the blue of the mountain bluebird. The dream blue.

He was beginning to fade. Or was it her eyes? They felt so heavy. It was a struggle to keep them open. Everything was a blur.

Stay awake. Keep talking. Power in. Fear out. "What's . . . your name?" she asked.

"My son. That's what Grandfather called me. And sometimes Jonathan."

Breathe in. Breathe out.

"Jonathan," she said. "Nice. It means 'God's gracious gift.'" All at once she found she could speak more easily. Or were the words simply flowing in her mind and not spoken out loud? Somehow she heard herself say, "I've got a book about names. My father's name is Ian and Ian's a variation of John, and John means 'God's gracious gift,' too. My aunt's name is Joanne, and her name means the same thing. My name is Ashley. It means 'a dweller in the ash-tree meadow.' It's in the boy's section of the book. I call my aunt, Jo. That's a boy's name, too. And my friend Erica, her name means 'royalty,' and Raven, he's got the name of a bird."

She was rambling but the boy didn't seem to notice. Perhaps she hadn't voiced the words out loud. He only seemed to have heard one thing. "Jonathan means a gift of God?" he said. A smile lit up his face. "What does it look like? They were going to sign me on at the railway but there wasn't time."

Ashley frowned. "I don't know what you mean."

"My name. I've never seen it."

"Oh . . . I'll show you." She printed his name in the snow, making each letter look bold and important. When she was finished, he traced over the letters with a finger, saying his name as he did so.

"Your grandfather," Ashley said. "What was his name?"

Jonathan gave her a funny look. "His name was Grandfather. Grandfather Silver. It should have been Gold since he worked with gold. Silver was my other name, too. Show me what Silver looks like."

She began to print again, naming each letter. "S L I V — no, that's not right." She changed the L to an I, the I to an L. "I do that all the time. Reverse the letters, get the words wrong — oh, my God!"

Suddenly she understood. "You're the sliver! I kept dreaming of a sliver, and I thought it was a splinter of wood or glass. But it wasn't sliver, it was silver. It was you."

An idea came to her. "Jonathan, I can give you your name. I can get you a new gravestone. You won't be unknown. You'll be Jonathan Silver."

He thought for a moment. "Can you put Grandfather's name on it, too?"

"Yes. I'll put Jonathan Silver and Grandfather. I'll do it right now."

"No, no. Not now," Jonathan said. "Everyone goes

away and leaves me. You're the Ashley I've been waiting for. I don't want you to go."

Ashley fought the rising panic, the feeling that she was lost. No one would find her, she would never escape, she would never go home.

Then the frantic beating of her heart slowed as she realized it wasn't really her that Jonathan had been waiting for, it was the goldstone. If she gave him the goldstone . . .

Give, take. Go, stay. Once again, that familiar tug.

She struggled to raise her arms. When had they become so heavy? With numb fingers, she unfastened the chain. Then she painstakingly removed the goldstone and placed it in front of the boy. "Keep . . . promise," she whispered. *Breathe in. Breathe out.* "Take the goldstone. But I want the chain. Family heirloom, like a promise. All right?"

She didn't wait for him to answer. She tried to lift her arms to refasten the chain but the effort was too great. Instead she placed it in her pocket.

The boy smiled at her and started to hum. It was the low, throbbing hum Ashley had heard a lifetime ago. This time she recognized the tune. The sound was soothing. Mesmerizing. It continued even as Jonathan faded away. Or was she the one who was fading? Was that what he meant by the shimmer?

Her eyes closed. Her head dropped to her chest. The snow folded in around her, and molded her into the dark.

42

At least Raven had a shovel. So if — no, *when* — they found Ashley, they'd be able to dig her out.

It had been a present from his father the previous Christmas, a small shovel with a strong blade and short removable handle, small enough to fit inside his pack. They'd joked about it at the time, him and Dad. Raven laughing, "What a crummy present! You just want me to do work. And look at the size of the handle! You think I'm going to shovel your driveway with this toy?" And Dad saying, "If you're coming into the backcountry with me, you might need it. I want to know there's somebody who can dig me out. There's something else, too. See the gift certificate taped to the scoop? It's for that avalanche safety course. You never know . . ."

Raven had stopped listening. One phrase danced in his head. *If you're coming with me . . .* "You mean it, Dad? You're taking me into the backcountry?"

Sure, Dad had meant it. For twenty minutes. The time it took to buy the shovel and wrap it up. Maybe he hadn't even done that. Maybe he'd been seeing Misty What's-Her-Face way back then and got her to do it. She'd phoned the recreation center, got the certificate mailed out, bought the shovel, picked out the jolly reindeer wrapping paper. Maybe her and Dad'd had a good laugh over Raven's anticipated reaction. What, not a computer game? Not a snowboard? Why, it's a shovel! Ya-hoo.

It ended up being Ashley's dad who'd taken Raven into the backcountry. And they'd always had shovels, just in case.

Up . . . forward . . . down.

They had now reached the spot where Ashley had last been seen. They'd found one of her skis, both poles, her ski hat, and mittens.

"What now, Raven?" Clipper turned to his friend, an anxious expression scrawled across his face. The others stared at Raven and waited. Everyone looked exhausted and despondent.

Raven pushed the hair out of his eyes and swallowed hard. Why me? Who made me the leader? In what he hoped was a confident voice, he said, "We go down and make another pass. But we should move the line over a bit to the left."

They marked the new boundary and started again.

Up . . . forward . . . down.

How much time had passed? How much time did they have left?

Raven tried not to think. Maybe he was wrong, maybe someone should've gone for help. Maybe a rescue team could've got there in time with proper probes and dogs, and Ashley would've been found. One more pass, he decided. Then someone can go for help while the rest of us keep probing.

Up . . . forward . . . down.

"I've got something!" Steph's voice broke into his thoughts, quiet at first, then growing loud with excitement. "Raven, you guys, I've got something!" She dropped her pole and frantically began digging with her hands.

"Wait, Steph, I'll do it with the shovel." Raven dug down until he felt the blade hit against something. "Oh, God. Oh, please, please, I think this is it . . ." A moment later he cried in despair, "Oh, no!" And pulled out Ashley's pack.

It was worse than before.

That moment of hope. The overwhelming relief. Then nothing.

Had they missed her? Was she buried too deep? Was she more to the left? Or to the right?

Up . . . forward . . . down.

"Wait . . . I think, I think I've hit something." Scout, this time. His voice was cautious. He probed again in the same spot. "Should it feel soft? Sort of cushiony?"

Raven inserted his pole. "This could be it," he said. He forced himself to stay calm. Angle in, shovel the snow, toss it away, shovel again, and when she's out, if it's really her, then we'll see . . .

"It's her, it's her!" Erica cried. "Ashley, oh, God!"

Raven, still digging, three feet down, held his breath until he uncovered the back of Ashley's head. Digging gently, careful not to cut with the blade, he saw she was curled up in a fetal position, her hands cupped around her face. "Ohhh . . . oh, thank God!" His breath came in gasps, his chest ached with a pain he'd never felt before. Slow down, he told himself. Take it easy, it's not over yet.

"Looks like she had an air space," Scout said. "That's a good sign."

"Does it look like she's breathing?" Steph said. "She's, she's so white, so frozen and stiff. She looks —" Her voice broke off in a sob.

The others knew what she was thinking. No one could say the word.

"Look," Clipper said. "I'll go to the trailhead, and if I don't run into a park warden or somebody, I'll go down the highway to the warden's office. We're going to need blankets and a toboggan to get her out."

"Break tree branches so you'll know exactly how to get back here!" Raven called as Clipper set off. "And hurry!"

Erica kneeled in the snow and put her fingers against the artery in Ashley's neck. "She's probably unconscious, that's all, so there has to be a pulse. I can't feel it, though, I can't feel anything. Raven, you try."

Raven pressed his fingers on Ashley's neck and held them for several seconds. "I think I feel something. It's faint, but I think — we have to do artificial respiration, mouth-to-mouth. Has anybody ever done it?"

"I got a badge for that," Scout said. "Move over, Raven. Let me try." He put his mouth over Ashley's and breathed in warm air from his own lungs.

She'll be cold, Raven kept thinking. She'll be so cold. He went back to digging out the snow, freeing her body little by little. The others helped dig with their hands, while Scout kept on with the artificial respiration. Finally he started to yell, "I've got a breath! She's breathing. Come on, Ashley! Come on!"

Ashley's eyelids fluttered open. She began to cough.

"She's breathing, she's conscious. C'mon, get her out!"

Raven, with Scout's help, gently lifted her out of the snow. "She's shivering like crazy," he said. "She needs warm clothes. Anybody got extras?"

"I've got dry socks and another sweater," Erica said, "but anything in our packs is going to be too cold. We've got to give her what we're wearing. You guys turn around."

The boys looked away while Erica removed Ashley's clothing and replaced it with her own thermal underwear, fleece top, and jacket. Steph helped by switching her warm ski pants with Ashley's cold ones and putting her two pairs of fleece socks on Ashley's feet. They tried to hurry in the cold.

As Erica was putting on Ashley's jacket, she noticed the gold chain hanging out of the pocket. She removed it, and saw that the goldstone was missing. "Did anybody see her goldstone? It's come off the chain."

"The avalanche must've ripped it off," Steph said. "Along with her mitts and hat. It's probably buried somewhere but we can't look now." She quickly finished dressing.

Raven gave Ashley his neck gaiter, pulled his ski hat down over her ears, and put his warm mittens on her frozen hands. "Anybody got anything else they can spare? Wrap whatever extra you've got around her. OK, Ashley? You see what we're doing?"

Ashley's eyes were open but unfocused, as if she were somewhere else. She didn't seem to recognize anyone, or even notice what was going on. Between spasms of shivering she kept muttering, "Silver, sliver," and half-singing, "Hush little baby, don't say a word . . ."

"What's she talking about?" Erica wondered.

"It's a song," said Steph. "You know. 'Hush little baby, don't say a word, Mama's gonna buy you a mockingbird.'"

"Yeah, but why? And what's with the silver?"

"I don't know, she's delirious. How intelligent would you sound if you'd been buried by an avalanche?"

"I'll give you the goldstone . . . Keep your promise, can't have the chain . . ."

"She's confused," Raven said. "She's probably got hypothermia."

"Maybe we should rub her arms?" said Steph. "Would that help get her warm?"

Scout shook his head. "She's in shock. And even if she's cold you're not supposed to rub her arms or legs

217

'cause that only moves the cold blood into the heart. I got a badge, we learned that in first aid. Has anybody got something for her to drink? Something hot?"

"I've got a thermos of hot Gatorade," Erica said, fishing inside her pack. "You know my mother. 'You gotta keep warm, you gotta keep warm.' But I never drank it at lunch, only cold soda." She poured some Gatorade into her cup and held it to Ashley's lips. "Take a sip, Ash. You got some? Great. And a bit more . . ."

"We should try to move her," Steph said. "We'll probably meet Clipper coming back with help, don't you think? We shouldn't just stand around here."

Scout agreed. "I saw this other thing on TV, where you make a sort of toboggan with skis and poles. Hey! Like Raven's doing. Good thinking, Rave! You need more straps? You can use the ones on my backpack."

"This should do it." Raven gave the four skis he'd strapped together a tug. "Put Ashley on top of this, but be careful."

They laid Ashley on the improvised toboggan, while Steph tied her scarf to the skis. "It's not the greatest, but at least we can pull it. Are we ready, then?"

"Let's go," said Raven.

They hadn't gone two feet when a voice cried, "What're you guys doing? I can walk!"

Everyone stopped and stared. "Ashley?"

"I think so," she said.

Erica knelt down in the snow and hugged her. "We're so glad you're back."

"I've been gone, haven't I? Not far, but I'm awfully

tired . . ." Then she burst out, "My mitts! And my hat! Where are they? Did I leave them in the cabin?"

Raven and the others looked at each other. Was it possible Ashley didn't know what had happened? "They must've fallen off," Raven said cautiously. "You know, the force . . ."

"Oh. The avalanche. It came after the lightning, didn't it? After the grandfather, and long after the lightning. I should've stayed home, you know. I saw it all in a dream, only it wasn't the boy that got buried, it was me. Well, he got buried, too, but that was a long time ago. And Karin couldn't save him . . ." Her eyes welled up with tears.

"Hey, girl!" Erica made an attempt to sound hearty. "You're in good shape, no broken bones that I can tell. Not that I'm a doctor, but hey! I was a pretty good nurse, getting you to drink stuff and everything, and you should have seen Scout with the mouth-to-mouth rescue. No kidding! And you — oh, God." She started to cry. "Ashley, we were so scared."

"Me too," Ashley murmured and reached out for another hug.

When they were about to start off again, Ashley was more insistent. "I can walk, honest! See? I can move my arms and legs."

"You were unconscious," Raven said firmly. "You're not supposed to walk if you've been unconscious."

"Do you know this for a fact? Look, I'm OK! I walked all the way to the cabin, which is practically on top of the Glacier and — oh."

"What are you talking about?"

"Nothing. I'm just tired."

They met the park wardens halfway down. Ashley was surprised to see that her dad was with them, but she didn't have the energy to ask why.

"Oh, honey," he exclaimed, "thank God you're all right!" He hugged her, his face expressing both shock and relief. Then he wrapped her in blankets, placed her on a litter, and gave her some hot chocolate.

"I'm sorry," she managed to say. "For causing so much trouble. If it hadn't been for Jonathan . . . But he did what he had to do. It's important, keeping a promise."

Raven and Erica exchanged glances. "Jonathan?" Raven said. "What's she talking about now?"

Erica shrugged. "I guess she's still delirious."

Then Ashley said something even more puzzling. She looked directly at Raven and said, "Jonathan was right. A raven showed him the way."

43

Ashley was fine.

The doctor gave her a thorough examination and said she was one lucky trooper. No internal injuries, nothing more serious than a mild case of hypothermia. He kept her in the hospital for a day, then sent her home for plenty of warmth and rest.

"It was Jo's doing," Dad said when Ashley asked how he'd ended up on the trail. "She was positive you were in danger. So I finally decided to go just to prove there was nothing to worry about. I got to the parking lot just as the wardens were heading out. Clipper was there, Matt Godfrey, and the others. They told me what happened. And when they said an ambulance was on its way — well, you can imagine how sick I felt. If I'd got there sooner . . ."

Ashley squeezed his hand. She didn't tell him it wouldn't have made a difference.

"The strange thing is," he went on, "everybody agrees there's no way that that particular avalanche could have happened under normal circumstances. No one can understand it."

Jo understood. Ashley had given her Karin's diary to read. "What was it Karin wrote?" she said. "'A mysterious force is at work in the mountains.'"

Ashley nodded. "I'm sorry . . . about giving away the goldstone."

"It's fine," Jo said and gave her a reassuring smile.

Since Ashley was supposed to rest, her mother wouldn't allow more than one visitor a day. So her friends took turns visiting, promising they'd have a big celebration when Ashley was well enough to go back to school.

"I'll no sooner be back than I'll be gone again," she reminded Erica. "I'm going to Australia, remember."

"So we'll have a Bon Voyage party at the same time. God, Ashley. Look at all the cards you've got. And presents! And flowers! Some people get all the luck."

"Erica!" Ashley was astounded. "You think I was *lucky*? To get hit by an avalanche?"

"No, no, I didn't mean — you're lucky you're alive, that's what I meant. If I hadn't gone off after Raven, if I'd stayed with you —"

"Sure, Erica. Then we could've been wiped out together."

"Yeah! Then I could've got rescued, too! Just like Snow White, eh, Ash? Only instead of coming to life with a kiss, it was mouth-to-mouth respiration. And naturally Scout isn't a prince. But still. Do you remember that part?"

"Hardly!" she laughed. "Good thing it wasn't Raven. You probably wouldn't even be talking to me." Then, in case Erica took her remarks the wrong way, she added, "He really does like you, you know."

Erica beamed.

"Anyway, I hardly get *all* the luck. It's spring break, remember? I don't even miss any school."

The following morning Raven arrived with a cluster of multicolored balloons, so large he could hardly make it through the doorway.

"Wow!" Ashley exclaimed. "Here, tie them to my desk chair, if it can stay on the ground. How many are there? Ten, no twelve! You biked over here with *twelve* balloons?"

Raven blushed and grinned self-consciously. "I know I looked pretty stupid. I tied them to my handle-bars, and they kept blowing back and swatting me in the face. But I wanted — you like them?"

"I love them, you goof! They're beautiful."

He blushed a deeper shade of red. "I wanted to say — you know, when we were skiing, I should've —"

Ashley sighed with impatience. "It wasn't your fault! Jeez, Raven. I don't get it. Everybody thinks it was *their* fault. You, Erica, my dad, my aunt. All I hear is, 'If I'd done this, if I hadn't done that . . .' You know what? If it's anybody's fault, it's mine. I dreamed the whole thing. I should've known better than to go in the first place. I just didn't understand the signs. I'm really good at my aunt's rhyming codes, but the dreams! Talk about cryptic. You were a part of it, too, you know. Not in my dream, but in Jonathan's. And he got confused, same as me. What he thought was a bird raven, was really you."

"Who? What? Have you completely lost your mind?"

"Just listen, all right? Then you can decide."

There was a long silence after Ashley had finished her story. Then Raven said, "There's a rational explanation and some day I'll figure it out. But right now —" he broke off and laughed. "When you interrupted me awhile ago, I was never going to say it was my fault. Heck, I know it wasn't! What I wanted to say was — when we were out skiing, that whole day — until the avalanche, I mean — all I could think about was how much I hated my dad and that person he's going to marry. And I should've just let it go. Like, months ago. It was such a waste of thought! And taking it out on everybody else. I mean, even if Dad's a — a whatever, he's still my dad. And I'll just hafta see how it goes." He let out a long breath. "Whew! Is your dad around?"

"Outside, I think. Putting up some new bird feeders, polishing his binoculars, flexing his wings . . ."

Raven laughed. "See ya, then."

As Ashley watched him shrug into his jacket she thought how unlike Raven it was to have confided in her the way he had. It must've taken some courage, and she couldn't help but be pleased. All the same, she felt there was something missing, something left unsaid. He was halfway out the door when she realized what it was. "Hey, Raven. Aren't you forgetting something?"

He turned with a look of sheer horror on his face, as if afraid she might be expecting a hug or a kiss.

"Don't look so worried," she laughed. "I just realized, this is the first time I've ever spent more than ten minutes with you, when you haven't reeled off one single trivial fact. It's amazing! Don't you know anything about hypothermia? Or balloons? Or helium?"

He grinned. "I'm saving it up for the next time."

At the end of spring break Ashley went back to school with the others. On her way home that first day, she stopped by the museum. She was pleased to see that her mother had made a display of Karin's wildflower sketches, but that wasn't why she'd come. "Mom, can I look through the stuff about the Rogers Pass avalanche?"

Her mother looked surprised. "Anything specific?"

"That memorial card you showed me once. The one that has the names on it. Of the men who died."

Mom went downstairs and came back with a bulging file folder. "Have a look through here."

Ashley quickly found what she was looking for. It was a card, edged in black, from the memorial service held in Revelstoke after the avalanche. Reading through the long list of names, she saw one that she recognized. It was Charles Anderson, her great-grand-father's younger brother. There was no mention of a Jonathan Silver.

But of course there wouldn't be. He'd already told her they hadn't known his name.

She looked through some other papers to pass the time while waiting for Mom to finish work. Photographs, newspaper clippings, letters, all dealing with the terribly tragedy at Rogers Pass.

Some letters had been written by people from as far away as Belfast and London. There were letters from relatives asking if So-and-So, last known to be working for the railway in British Columbia, had been killed in the slide. If so, could his belongings be returned?

There were lists of personal effects found on some of the bodies, with requests for the next-of-kin to come forward and claim them. Things like watches, rings, cigarette lighters, articles of clothing . . .

Ashley scanned over several such lists, then stopped. This could be it. *Boots, undershirt, vest, drawers . . .* " Mom, what are drawers?"

"Drawers, as in clothing? They're what we call long johns."

Ashley read on. *Tan gloves, lined with wool. Fur cap. Blue denim overalls. Heavy winter working shirt, medium gray. Blue mackinaw with hood, one button missing. Two white handkerchiefs. Red glass marble.* "It's him," she said. "I've found Jonathan Silver."

It took longer to find the gravestone. After searching for an hour, Ashley found what she was looking for. It was in a far corner of the cemetery and had sunk so deep into the earth it was barely visible. Weeds grew around it, and years of mildew and moss had discolored the surface. The letters were no longer as clearly etched as they had once been, but there was no mistaking the word on the gravestone.

"He really was unknown," Ashley said quietly. "Everything he said was true." How sad, to be so alone in the world that when you died, nobody knew or cared.

But she knew. And strangely enough, she cared. The goldstone had created a link between her and the boy, a link that had touched not only her life, but the lives of Auntie Jo and Karin. "I made him a promise," she said. "To have his name put on the gravestone. Can we do that?"

Mom gave her a hug. "Of course we can. We'll have it done before you leave."

"All's well that end's well," Dad said as they were leaving the cemetery.

"Not quite, Dad." Ashley touched the chain around her neck. It would be a long while before she stopped missing the goldstone.

44

Perth, Western Australia
May 11

Dear Mom and Dad,

Guess what? I'm in your tomorrow and you're still in my yesterday. It's fair dinkum great being ahead for once!!

We just got back to Perth after spending the weekend in Bindoon, where Auntie Jo has her bush block. That's what she calls it. It's a cabin with five acres of slivery eucalyptus trees and wonderful feathery plants and hundreds of black cockatoos and red-capped parrots and kookaburras that wake you at dawn! And in the field nearby there are wild kangaroos!!!

Guess what? We're going down the coast tomorrow, all the way to Augusta, where Auntie Jo saved the whales. Dad, I'll send you a postcard!! Except you'll be here pretty soon to see it yourself.

I have to go now because we're making a fruit salad for supper. Auntie Jo keeps saying the mangos must be eaten! Then I have to e-mail Raven and Erica.

You're really, really going to love it here. Wait till you see the birds!!! See you next week.

Love, Ashley

She read over her letter, turned on the modem, and pressed SEND. *Whishh!* Her words vanished into cyberspace. Soon, way back in yesterday, Mom or Dad would flick a switch and retrieve her message. Like magic.

She shut down the computer, and as she was getting up, happened to catch her reflection in the blank screen. The gold chain glittered at her throat.

She wondered if anyone had found the goldstone. It was still too early for spring melt, but someone skiing in the park might have seen it glistening against the snow. Someone might have picked it up, cleaned it, and put it on a chain. Maybe someone, right this minute, was asleep and dreaming the future. Or maybe someone was wearing it as a pendant, little knowing of the magic inside.

In the summer she'd get a group together, Mom and Dad and her friends, and she'd lead them to Jonathan's cabin. She was certain she'd be able to find it. Maybe the goldstone would still be there, right where she'd left it. If it was . . .

Ashley laughed out loud. What was she thinking? The goldstone wouldn't be there. Neither would the cabin. You can't go back inside a dream.

The goldstone was buried in the avalanche. She had no idea what would become of it when the snow melted, or if it would ever be found. Maybe that was for the best. It was where it belonged, where Jonathan wanted it to be. In the snow, in the mountains, in the shadow of the Glacier.

45

The time of the Ashley was over.

Jonathan had known this as he watched her disappear from his world back into her own.

His search for the goldstone was over, too. It lay safely buried beneath the snow, close enough to Grandfather to count as a promise well-kept.

The Ashley had kept her promise. The names *Jonathan Silver and Grandfather* were carved on the gravestone, but even with the names, Jonathan didn't like the place they'd made for him. And so he returned to the mountains.

All time was over. Before and after the lightning, before and after the avalanche.

Jonathan knew this, as he shimmered for the last time.

One bright glow, then into the space between fire and ice.

And Grandfather's voice, calling him to the shadow of the Glacier, where a late spring snow was beginning to fall.